The Accidental Diary of **B.U.G.**

BASICALLY FAMOUS

Jen Carney

PUFFIN

PUFFIN BOOKS

UK | USA | Canada | Ireland | Australia
India | New Zealand | South Africa

Puffin Books is part of the Penguin Random House group of companies
whose addresses can be found at global.penguinrandomhouse.com.

www.penguin.co.uk
www.puffin.co.uk
www.ladybird.co.uk

First published 2021
001

Text design by Janene Spencer
Printed in Great Britain by Clays Ltd, Elcograf S.p.A.

The authorized representative in the EEA is Penguin Random House Ireland,
Morrison Chambers, 32 Nassau Street, Dublin D02 YH68

A CIP catalogue record for this book is available from the British Library

ISBN: 978–0–241–45547–0

All correspondence to:
Puffin Books
Penguin Random House Children's
One Embassy Gardens, 8 Viaduct Gardens, London SW11 7BW

For my three musketeers, JJ, EV and IZ —
if you can dream it, you can achieve it

HELLO!
(AND POTENTIALLY GOODBYE . . .)

Hello! My name is **B**elinda **U**pton **G**reen (yes, yes, that's the 'Bug' bit — move on) and this is my second STAY-AWAKE DOODLE **DIARY**.

NOT AT ALL SAD

S.A.D. DIARY

I'm extra pleased you're thinking of reading it, but before you start gloating about finally getting your hands on one of the best books in your class library, I'm afraid I must issue a SERIOUS WARNING. It is UTTERLY UNSUITABLE for some people.

With that in mind, I have developed a foolproof ARE YOU DEFINITELY THE RIGHT KIND OF PERSON TO CONTINUE READING THIS AWESOME BOOK? experiment for which I insist you prepare immediately. Don't worry — I won't be requiring a sample of your wee or anything; gurning into a mirror for seventeen seconds, licking your elbows or speed-eating a couple of custard creams should do it.

Warmed up? PERFECT! You have my permission to start. (Eek! I'm crossing my fingers for you.)

INSTRUCTIONS:
From each pair of pictures, simply choose **A** or **B** as fast as you can. OK?
On your marks . . . get set . . .

GOALIE! (Sorry . . . couldn't resist.)
ONYOURMARKSGETSETGO!

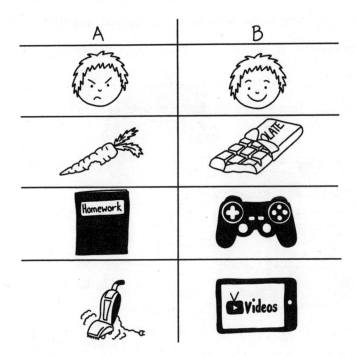

	A	B
	(angry face)	(smiling face)
	(carrot)	(chocolate bar)
	Homework	(game controller)
	(vacuum cleaner)	Videos

Well done. Now let me analyse your answers using my (un)tried and (barely) tested 'hardly ever wrong' machine . . .

While you're waiting for your answers to be processed, may I suggest this completely normal and not-at-all-embarrassing waiting-room activity? Shout 'I! DONE! UP! WHO!' ten times as fast as you can.

OK, stop — people are staring. (And look: your results are in . . .)

MOSTLY As: We have encountered an error with your answers. Please restart your brain and try again. If the problem persists, go out and buy some carrots, then ask your teacher for extra homework.

MOSTLY Bs: You are 100% the right type of reader for this book. Reward yourself with a biscuit and twelve minutes' screen time while you prepare for a laugh.

YIPPEE! I knew you'd make it through. I hereby reward you with a mini animation.

FLIP HERE

Right, on with the book for real! I have some exciting news to share already!

EXCITING NEWS

ONE MORE THING . . .

For the benefit of anyone who hasn't read my
first diary, I just want to say:

PLEASE DON'T PANIC!

I'm a **total expert** in helping people get up to
date on essential details in record time. Today,
for example, it took me under three minutes
to update my **#BBF**, Dale Redman,
on a whole hour-long maths
lesson he'd missed. In fact,
you know what, if I was Class
Five's permanent teacher,
I'm certain I could fit a full
week's worth of learning

#BBF (BEST
BOY FRIEND)

ESSENTIAL SPACE ----

into about twenty-five minutes, leaving plenty of time for chatting and inventing new games (which annoyingly I have to **squeeze** into our daily spelling-challenge time nowadays).

Here goes — a rundown of 'you probably should know this before you start' stuff:

1. I'm ten and I'm a terribul speller, an epic game maker-upperer and an OK doodler.

2. I'm the leader of TOBLA (**T**he **O**fficial **B**iscuit **L**aw **A**ssociation).

3. My 100% #BFF is Layla Dixon.

#BFF (BEST FRIEND FOREVER)

See what I mean about being the best catcher-upperer ever? I still suggest any newbies read my first diary so you can discover the juicier details from the last few weeks of my life (spoiler alert: I caught an ACTUAL THIEF single-handedly). But I'm not going to force you or anything. Forced reading is my number-two hate.

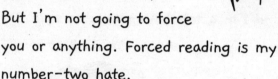

SHE'S A BIT OF A CATCHER-UPPER . . .

THINGS I HATE
1. SPELLINGS
2. FORCED READING
3. PEOPLE WITH NARROW MINDS
4. 'NICE' BISCUITS
5. ASSEMBLIES

Oh, and if you're wondering what's so accidental about my diaries . . . I have a habit of 'accidentally' using my SPELLINGS jotters to write them. OOPS.

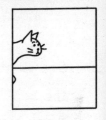

100% SECRET FROM MY PARENTS. SHH.

OK, let's get down to business.

PEEING IN CLASS

After assembly today, Mrs Patterson announced, at the top of her voice, that we were going to

be 'LEARNING ABOUT PEE!' To be completely truthful, she actually said 'PEE comments', but most of us, as you can imagine, laughed our heads off before we'd heard the 'comments' bit.

Sadly these piddly-named remarks turned out to be nothing whatsoever to do with talking about

the colour or smell of your WEE. That
would've been 100% more interesting
than listening to our teacher ramble on
for an hour about Point-Evidence-Explanation —
yet another new writing rule Class Five
must try to use.

Although the lesson was duller than a rich tea
biscuit, its conclusion cracked me up.
'Now remember, children,'
said Mrs Patterson
before letting us out
for break, 'you should
practise PEE-ing in
your reading records
on a regular basis!'

I've not brought my reading record to bed
(obviously — I'm not completely INSANE). But,
as Mrs 'P' (!) threatened that anyone who can't
PEE properly by Friday will have to STAY IN at

lunchtime for one-to-one SUPPORT, I've decided to practise PEE-ing in my diary. Sorry if it gets a bit messy!

P(OINT): Metal detectors are quite possibly THE. BEST. THINGS. EVER. (Not including screen time, biscuits, being chosen to be register monitor and snow days.)

E(VIDENCE): I know this because I've had mine for two weeks and already it has:

a. enabled me to pack in my day job. Detecting dropped coins on the field behind our house after tea is far more interesting (and occasionally more ~~loocrativ~~ ~~lou=cr=tiv~~ rewarding) than emptying the dishwasher for 20p.

b. dramatically improved my TREASURE CLUB contributions. Although even my collection of multicoloured metal bottle lids didn't manage to beat the oversized paperclip Dale brought in

last week (that he'd expertly bent
into the shape of Australia).

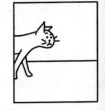

AND

c. got me an invitation to search for DEAD MAN'S
   GOLD! (This is my exciting news, by the way.)

E(XPLANATION): Hmm . . . I'm not exactly sure
what I'm supposed to write here. By this point
in the yawnsome lesson I'd stopped listening to
Mrs Patterson in favour of continuing my list of
'words that can easily be drawn'. So I'm going
to have to leave PEE-ing
there for now. Oh well,
I can always try
wangling the seat next
to Elliot when it
comes to Friday's
PEE-ing test.

WORDS THAT CAN
EASILY BE DRAWN

1. PANETTONE
2. DIVERSITY
3. CROAKING
4. RUGBY

ELIOT AKA
BRAINBOX

DEAD MAN'S GOLD

Sorry if you thought I was going to go to sleep without sharing my exciting news. I just had to be sure my parents are in bed (they are — I've made two fake toilet trips to double-check). Well, I can't have my second STAY—AWAKE DOODLE DIARY 'SPELLINGS jotter' confiscated on its very first day of existence, can I?! I'll have to be brief, though. It's already 10.30 p.m.

Basically, as Mum and I walked Mr Paws after school today, we saw a little old woman drop to her knees and grope around the base of a poo bin with her bare hands. As that's not the usual way people round here pick up their dogs' business,

and because Mum's a trained first-aider, we dashed over to check she was OK. She wasn't.

However, it wasn't **Mum's** life-saving skills she needed; it was MINE!

She'd dropped her house keys while removing a poo bag from her pocket, you see, and my metal detector turned out to be MILES more useful than

the mini first-aid kit my mum insists on carrying in her pocket every time we leave the house.

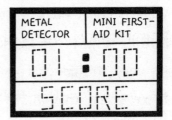

METAL DETECTOR	MINI FIRST-AID KIT
01 : 00	
SCORE	

The woman's name was Gracie Seagull. She smelled of lavender and had the LOUDEST, poshest voice I've ever heard. 'Oh, lovie!' she BOOMED when I reunited her with her keys. 'Thank you ever so much. You're a real LIFESAVER.'

THEN SHE GAVE ME 50P!

I'm not exactly sure whether this was a reward for saving her life or for finding her keys. Either

way, it means I'm now only 26p off being able
to afford the limited-edition bumper pack of
CHOCOLATE custard creams Mum refused to let

me put in our trolley
last week. (Which I
downright disagree will
just be 'Bourbons with a fancy name
and a hefty price tag'.)

Anyway . . . after that, we chatted about our
dogs who, as Gracie Seagull said, appeared to
have 'fallen in love at first bum-sniff'!

Honestly, for an old woman she was extra funny.
She reminded me of my great-nan. I mean, she
didn't do THUNDEROUS TRUMPS or show me her
false teeth or anything, but she was equally

enthusiastic about engaging in a full-body scan. I went straight in for the kill, aiming my metal detector at her hip, and suspected I'd hit the jackpot when I heard a faint bleep. I was spot on. Gracie dug deep into her coat pocket and offered me a mint! It's my new party trick — old people ALWAYS have a cylinder of sweet treats secreted about their person and, nine times out of ten, they're wrapped in foil.

MINT

AKA
MINT-FINDER

ASTONISHED by the power of my metal detector, Gracie asked me whether I'd ever found anything valuable. When I mentioned GOLD (not a lie — I located the back of a gold earring last week) her beady eyes lit up. Gathering her little dog close to her face, she proceeded to tell us a long story about her 'late' husband who, many years ago, lost his valuable gold wedding ring while weeding their garden.

And by 'late', BTW, she meant 'dead' — which I rather wish she'd made clear at the start of her tale. I mean, how was I to know? I thought she was crying because her husband never arrived at parties on time . . .

MAYBE YOU SHOULD CALL HIM 'CARELESS' INSTEAD OF 'LATE'!?

Anyway . . . when I mentioned how we'd **love** to see if my metal detector was up to the job of finding the late ring, Gracie Seagull gave Mum her phone number and said, if we ever fancied a challenge, she'd be DELIGHTED to see us again!

ALTHOUGH I DON'T FANCY YOUR CHANCES AFTER FIFTEEN YEARS!

So there you go — I'm *in no way* exaggerating when I say I've been invited to search for DEAD MAN'S GOLD.

PS I've just read what I've written about Gracie Seagull. If '**helping old people find lost gold**' (which I might be able to borrow for TREASURE CLUB) is not a fair E(xplanation) of why owning a metal detector is completely AWESOME, I don't know what would be. Maybe I'll be OK PEE-ing without Elliot's help on Friday.

YAY!

TREASURE CLUB

I called an emergency TREASURE CLUB meeting
at playtime today so I could share my exciting
news.

There are currently three and a half members in
TREASURE CLUB: Me (obvs), Layla (my #BFF),
Dale (our #BBF) and, if she's not too busy doing
the splits, Janey McVey (our #VBF). Some of
you might already know this but Janey McVey
only joined Class Five fairly recently. At first she
was a MEGA PEST who tried to steal Layla off me
and thought making mean comments would make
people like her. That's all behind us now and, at
the moment, we're friends. Not **V**ery **B**est
Friends, by the way (she's
still an annoying show-off
a lot of the time). VB
stands for Very Bendy.

Anyway, Dale and Layla totally freaked
out when I told them about DEAD MAN'S
GOLD. They're desperate to get involved.

I said I'd ask Mum to ask Gracie when she gets
round to calling her. Unfortunately, I'm not sure
Mum understands the URGENCY of this mission (or
the real meaning of the word 'soon'). I mean, it's
been over twenty-four hours now. How hard is it
to punch a few numbers into a phone and say,
'We'll come round tonight if that's OK'? On the
plus side, I know from experience that Mum's
SOONs are generally more reliable than her MAYBEs
or WE'LL SEEs so I'm still feeling optimistic.

Janey McVey didn't attend the emergency
TREASURE CLUB meeting. She decided that

showing Farida Banerjee how to do a handstand without using a wall was more urgent than hearing about DEAD MAN'S GOLD. So I was a bit cross with Layla when she spilled the full details at dinner break. Janey's response: 'Well, I found an emerald on my way to school this morning. I'll probably win TREASURE CLUB this week anyway.'

Then, in her typical 'I'll now ruin your AMAZING story further' way, she tried to suggest Gracie calling me a lifesaver was 'obviously ~~a mettafour metafore~~ one of those things people say when they're trying to be dramatic'. I mean, I know that's possible, but how does Janey know one of the million key rings dangling off Gracie's bunch wasn't a teeny-tiny life-saving medicine container? HMPH.

POSSIBLE LIFE-SAVING MEDICINE

If Janey's **genuinely** found an emerald, I **must** find DEAD MAN'S RING before Friday. All I've got so far this week is a rusty bent brooch I detected in Grandma Jude's button tin at the weekend. I'm not even sure whether it's a mole or a hedgehog, so I doubt it'll gain me the CHAMPION—FINDER title. But actual gold? That'd beat emerald, right? And surely Gracie's late-dead husband

is in no position to object to me borrowing it for a day as a reward for my super-finding skills . . .

Back in a sec . . .

AFTER FIFTEEN YEARS, ONE MORE DAY WON'T HURT . . .

R.I.P.
GRACIE'S HUSBAND

Sorry about that — I nipped to ask Mum about Dale and Layla coming to help on our quest (and to see if she's phoned Gracie yet). She said:

HMPH.

WATCHING YOUTUBE
IN CLASS

After assembly today, Mrs Patterson announced that our next few English lessons would be taken up with a 'SPECIAL project' and that, if we work super hard, we'll be rewarded with an 'EXTRAORDINARY treat'.

As Mrs Patterson's last 'SPECIAL project' involved a considerable amount of spellings (disguised as cutting and sticking) and the 'treat' awarded to the winning table was a new glue stick, I dipped my chin and raised one eyebrow.

When she continued by explaining we were going to learn about 'marketing', however, I clapped my hands and cleared my throat —

a class SHOUTING competition sounded right up my street.

Sadly that wasn't the kind of marketing Mrs Patterson meant. She meant the one where you make posters and adverts to create MASSIVE hype about something (even if it's rubbish) to convince people to pause their lives while they dash to the shops to buy one.

Everyone nodded, fully expecting
Mrs Patterson to dish out the felt-tips,
when something UNBELIEVABLE happened.
She wheeled in **the iPad trolley** and let us
watch YouTube in pairs all morning!

I KNOW!!

Before today we hadn't used the school iPads
since the day Patrick North set every single
home screen to an enlarged image of his left
nostril. Patrick North is the biggest pest in Class
Five, BTW. He's the only person who still calls
me 'Bug', and he possesses the worst habits
ever. If he's not wiping his snotty
nose on his jumper cuff, he's
talking with his mouth full
(usually to tell tales for no
good reason).

PEST OF THE
CENTURY

Anyway . . . we were only allowed to watch certain clips today — adverts for boring stuff like toothpaste and super-mops, and we had to write a bunch of tiresome PEE notes, outlining what was particularly persuasive about each video, but, still, it was 100% better than learning a new spelling rule.

Dale and I were partners and our iPad somehow (when Dale kept pressing the 'see more like this' button) kept skipping ahead. Although this meant we didn't manage to finish PEE-ing about fish fingers, the consequence was TOTALLY worth it. Staying in a room full of iPads at playtime enabled us to

rewatch the awesome FROOT GOOP advert we'd 'accidentally' skipped ahead to.

At dinner break we tried to teach everyone else the ultra-fast FROOT GOOP lyrics, then set a challenge (join in if you want). The first person to be able to recite the whole FROOT GOOP song without making a single error wins a GIANT (home-made) bottle of the stuff!

FROOT GOOP!

(to be chanted as speedily as possible)

A hamster halved a honeydew,
a cheetah chopped some cherries,
a ferret threw in fifty figs,
a monkey mashed some berries.
They mixed it in the zebra's bowl,
and added lemonade,
ten segments of a tangerine,
and that's how FROOT GOOP's made.
FROOT GOOP! FROOT GOOP!
Drink it in a hula hoop!
FROOT GOOP! FROOT GOOP!
Swig it in a chicken coop!
FROOT GOOP! FROOT GOOP!
Have it while you loop-the-loop!
FROOT GOOP! FROOT GOOP!
Come along and join our troop!

The only person who wasn't at all interested in FROOT GOOP was Janey. She said she'd lost one of her scrunchies and couldn't possibly concentrate on learning 'some stupid fruit song' amid a 'national disaster'. More fool her.

PS Although Mrs Patterson's comments about Dale and my PEE-ing skills have left me worried about missing out on the (possible) 'EXTRAORDINARY treat' she mentioned, they did enable me to expand my 'words that can easily be drawn' list.

ABOMINABLE

SUSPICIOUS BEHAVIOUR

Both my mums were waiting in the yard to greet me after school today. Now I realize this doesn't sound remotely newsworthy, but I'm telling you it is.

I guess I should mention at this point — in case you're 1. particularly forgetful, or 2. a newbie reader — I have two mums. Their names are Sarah and Katie and, before you ask, they're BOTH my **real** mum and, yes, that is possible so don't get your knockers in a twist. (Ha ha, 'knockers' was a mistake — I meant 'knickers', obvs.) However, it amused me so much I've

KATIE

SARAH

decided to leave it in
and put it right at the
top of my brand-new
'*hilarious words*' list.

HILARIOUS
WORDS
1. KNOCKERS

As a double-mum
pick-up hasn't happened since my first day in
reception class, and as they were both wearing
fancy(ish) clothes **and** make-up, I wondered
what on earth was going on. So I began by
asking some casual questions. 'WHAT ON EARTH'S
GOING ON?' being my first.

HELLO
TO YOU TOO! After reminding me
of good greeting
manners, they told me they'd had a
day off together to go to a 'meeting'.

'**What meeting?**' I demanded, wondering why
I hadn't been informed of this important event
requiring two thirds of our family's attendance.

Well, you'd think I'd asked them to reveal the colours of their bras in the middle of the playground the way they glanced over their shoulders and SHUSHED me before requesting that I calmed down.

Next, they tried to convince me their meeting was 'nothing I'd be interested in'. Ha! As they're well aware, I'm **always** interested in **things** (especially when the **things** sound a little bit secret or none of my business). They followed up this lie by asking me if I'd like to go for an ice cream. I totally knew this was their way of distracting me from asking more questions, but in the interest of a GREY POO—MAKER (check out my first diary if you don't know what that is) I decided to drop the matter.

However, I have not forgotten it. In fact, I've come to the conclusion that there are just two

possible explanations for their
secretiveness:

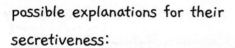

A. They didn't go to a meeting at all;
they pulled sickies from work to go shopping
for new bras or coat hangers or something
and (wrongly) assumed I wouldn't be
interested (or that I might ask for a treat).

B. They did attend a meeting, but it was with
some kind of holiday expert who helps newly
married couples get on with organizing their
honeymoon. And the reason why they're
acting so hush-hush is because
they're planning one of their
EPIC BIG REVEALS in a fancy
two-forked restaurant
(like they did before their
wedding when they
announced I was going
to be a bridesmaid).

I HAVE A
SURPRISE...

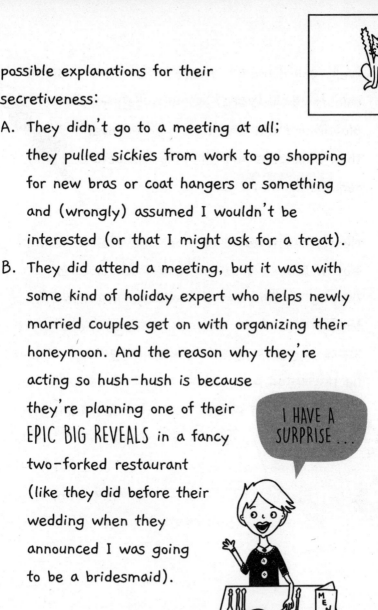

As I've discovered no evidence of new bras or coat hangers (yes, I looked), I'm convinced it was B. And, since they're obviously going to take me along, I hereby rename this future holiday our FAMILYMOON.

PS My 'molehog' brooch was voted 'second-best find of the week' at TREASURE CLUB today. Although I didn't win, I was extra pleased to beat Janey whose 'emerald' was, in fact, a tiny shard of green glass! Dale won **again**. This week he presented a key ring shaped like the Eiffel Tower that was also a torch! I suspect he'd 'found' this novelty attached to his grandad's car keys but, still, it sparked quite a conversation.

MATHS + GRAPHS = GRATHS

Writing about maths is not something I plan to waste this STAY–AWAKE DOODLE DIARY on (as I said, despite its nickname, it's in no way SAD). However, as today's lesson was about graphs and charts, I'm making an exception — particularly as it allowed me to conduct a BISCUIT SURVEY without Mrs Patterson accusing me of wasting my time.

I only gave people five options to choose from, but, even so, my findings might surprise you.

I felt sorry for custard creams. They're totally overlooked in the 'Epic Biscuits' arena.

That reminds me . . . On the very last page of my first (un)SAD Diary I promised to share some GOBSMACKING BISCUIT NEWS if my mum bought me another 'SPELLINGS jotter'. Sorry for the delay. Without further ado: Dale managed to sneak a Choc-A-Break into school last week. Now, as you might be aware, based on the insane and inflexible 'MORNING—BREAK SNACK MUST ALWAYS BE HEALTHY' rule at our school, that's news in itself. However, you won't believe the MASSIVENESS of the situation . . .

The Choc-A-Break contained NO wafer in one of its fingers. Honest! No wafer **AT ALL** . . . OMG. It was a digit of pure chocolate. Now I know if you were truly in the mood for a simple smallish chocolate treat, you could just buy one. But there's something ASTOUNDING about discovering a finger of NOTHING BUT

CHOCOLATE in a Choc-A-Break.

So, after we'd finished gazing at the mutant finger in total awe, Dale, Layla and I immediately drafted Biscuit Law number nine. Yes, yes, newbies, there are eight others (currently under consideration by the actual prime minister).

BISCUIT LAW 9: THE MALFORMED MUST
(this applies to awesomely mutant biscuits):
Thou shalt gloat gleefully, photograph the evidence and inform the newspapers before taking it to a museum for display (or enjoying it at your leisure).

Sorry. Where was I? . . . Oh yes, graths . . .

Layla created a bar chart to represent how many brothers and sisters Class Fivers have. She has three brothers and a brand-new baby sister called Neela, so she was the joint winner — with me. Janey McVey whined for ages to Mrs Patterson, trying to convince her I should be moved to the 'zero siblings' column (keeping her company). But if you have any pets you'll understand: Mr Paws and my three fish are **EXACTLY** like brothers and sisters.

After that, me and my #BFF worked together on a baby-poop pie chart. It totally helped channel Layla's current (weird) obsession with describing baby Neela's nappy contents.

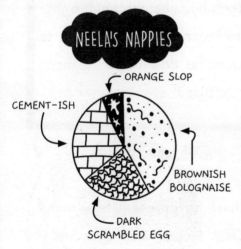

NEELA'S NAPPIES

ORANGE SLOP

CEMENT-ISH

BROWNISH BOLOGNAISE

DARK SCRAMBLED EGG

Maybe being an only child is for the best. Don't get me wrong — I get on extremely well with Neela (despite her attempting to ruin the most important day of my life recently by being born smack-bang in the

middle of it). But I couldn't cope living with a poo factory full-time.

In her typical 'look how much work I can do, Mrs Patterson' style, Janey 'No Brothers Or Sisters — Or Pets' McVey produced three graphs in the time most people managed one. First she made a bar chart about people's parents — just so she could SHOW OFF about being the only person in our class whose dad has a boyfriend. Then she made a line graph of weight and height — just to be nosy. Lastly she created a pie chart to illustrate which girls in Class Five could do the splits. However, because she'd spent so much time SNOOPING about how heavy everyone was, she only had time to add Layla's and my answers to her own . . .

CAN

CAN'T

ONE WORD, TWO MEANINGS

FINALLY!

Me and Mums went to Gracie Seagull's house today.

OMG. It was MASSIVE and uber old. From the outside, it looked like a rundown old hotel that'd be a perfect setting for a terrifying Halloween film. If Mums would just buy me my own iPad, I'd totally become an AWESOME movie director — after I'd completed *Biscuit-Maker* (a new game Painy McVey and Pestrick North constantly show off about owning and which, despite it sounding like it was made for me, Mum K refuses to download on her iPad).

Gracie's overgrown back

garden was virtually as big as our school field. I was desperate to explore it (and find the ring, of course) but Gracie had laid a little table with a pot of tea, a plate of scones and a jar of strawberry jam.

'Come and tell me more about yourselves, lovies,' she boomed, offering me the plate of scones.

As Mum K had only let me have a small banana after my tuna sandwich at lunchtime, I gave her my best smug glance, piled a MOUNTAIN of jam on the HUGEST scone of the lot, took an ENORMOUS bite and . . . immediately realized I had three problems:

1. The scone was CHEESE flavoured.
2. The jam was ONION chutney.
3. Mum was staring at me with her unsympathetic 'don't you dare' eyes.

Fortunately, Gracie Seagull is one of those extra-clever noticey people who spot secret-code stares. 'Oh, let her spit it out if she doesn't like it, lovie!' she said, handing me a napkin. Mums rolled their eyes at each other. Eagle-eyed Gracie noticed this too. 'Are you two sisters?' she asked.

This is a question old people often ask my mums, despite them looking NOTHING like each other. They never seem to tire of answering it, though. Mums explained how they're a married couple and I'm their daughter, then waited to see how Gracie would react. I closed my eyes and prayed she wasn't going to delay our ring-finding mission even further by needing a lesson about modern families.

Did I tell my new readers yet my mums adopted me when I was eight months old? Well, they did. And, if you don't know what that means,

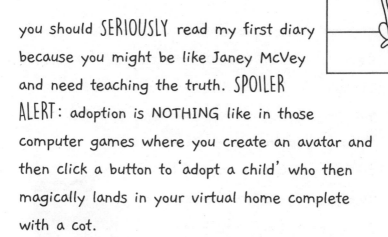

you should SERIOUSLY read my first diary because you might be like Janey McVey and need teaching the truth. SPOILER ALERT: adoption is NOTHING like in those computer games where you create an avatar and then click a button to 'adopt a child' who then magically lands in your virtual home complete with a cot.

This is not adoption either.

Anyway, Gracie proved she was an open-minded clever clogs. 'Oh, lovely,' she chirped. 'My son, Graham, is gay. He lives in Australia with his man friend, doesn't he, Clemency Boo-Boo Coochie-Coo?'

Clemency (Boo-Boo Coochie-Coo) didn't reply. She was more interested in sniffing some cheesy egg she'd found embedded on the side of my left trouser leg . . .

'Gay', by the way, is a word with two meanings. Gracie meant her son loves another man, not a woman. 'Gay' can also mean bright. 'Gay' is a word NO ONE at school is EVER allowed to use in a bad way. Once, last year, Liam Tabernacle (who thinks he's clever but who's actually mean and narrow-minded) called Elliot Quinn's new trainers 'gay'. He definitely didn't mean bright because they were black. Liam got into SO MUCH TROUBLE. His dad had to come in and everything.

DULL

Although 'gay' would be a good adjective to use in our writing, especially if we were talking about a lovely summer's day (or even a man who loves a man), everyone steers clear of it after the whole Liam—Elliot—trainer incident. It was a VERY BIG DEAL.

Hang on . . . Mum's doing her ear-to-the-door thing. How do I know? Because I can hear her whispering 'What on earth?' so I know her hair's stuck in the glue-stick smear I left on the door

for this exact purpose. Excuse me for a moment.
I suspect a room invasion is ~~iminent~~ ~~imanent~~
about to happen . . .

I
♥
SPELLINGS

IMPORTANT SPELLINGS FOR MY IMPORTANT SECOND SPELLINGS JOTTER

Homonyms are words that are spelled the same but mean different things. How many can you think of?

Sorry about that short interlude. Mum S wasn't pleased to see my torch on at 9.30 p.m. on a school night (or to get glue in her hair) but seeing me doing my spellings lightened her mood. She even said how DELIGHTED she was to see I'd filled so many pages of my new 'SPELLINGS jotter' already!

I'm afraid I'll have to finish telling you about Gracie's garden speedily, though; Mum's gone in the bathroom (and she didn't mention needing a poo).

Basically, after **a lot** more chatting, we got down to business. To cut a long story short, we didn't find the ring . . .

But it wasn't a complete waste of an afternoon. As well as seven random screws and a rusty trowel, my metal detector helped me to find £1.12, which Gracie let me keep! I also detected dozens of scraps of colourful metallic paper —

making me suspect Gracie and her early
husband (Ronnie) once enjoyed a tin of
Quality Street in their garden. Sounds
100% better than a cheesy-oniony picnic.

The good news is Gracie said I was welcome to
continue my search **any time**. I hope Dale and
Layla can tag along. GOLD—SEEKING definitely
feels like more of a TREASURE CLUB kind of
mission than a family one. Plus, I'm certain my
friends wouldn't spend the whole time saying

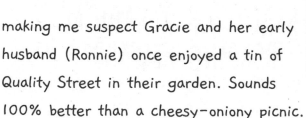

CAREFUL YOU
DON'T STEP ON THOSE
FLOWERS, BILLIE!

and

WATCH YOU DON'T
TRAMPLE THAT PLANT,
BILLIE!

like Mums did ~~threwout~~ ~~throo-out~~ all afternoon.

READY FOR A RADICAL READING REWARD?

Tired of books never giving you anything?

Brace yourself! Brilliance bounds before you! I'm not kidding — you're about to read the most MARVELLOUS diary entry I've EVER written. Not only does it come with a FREE bag of Haribo, it includes a special voucher granting you **a whole morning OFF lessons**, which your teacher is legally obliged to accept. **DO NOT** even *think* about skipping ahead. I mean it.

Our 'SPECIAL project' involved persuasive writing today. Apparently I'm SPECTACULAR at it. Mrs Patterson, whose compliments (to me) are as

rare as malformed biscuit discoveries,
even read my work aloud. So, although
it wasn't as fun as watching YouTube, it
did mean that I beat twenty-nine people today —
at English! (Which surely puts me back in the
running for the 'EXTRAORDINARY treat'.)

Everyone else, you see, had written their
persuasive letters in the opposite way to me —
basically trying to tempt Mr Epping (our droney-
onny head teacher) to ditch school uniform. The
thing is, Mr Epping is OBSESSED with school
uniform. He bangs on about
it frequently in morning
assemblies, particularly
the importance of wearing
'**regulation jumpers**' (ones
embroidered with our school
logo). So I knew that
writing such a paragraph
would be a pointless task.

THINGS I HATE
1. SPELLINGS
2. FORCED READING
3. PEOPLE WITH
   NARROW MINDS
4. 'NICE' BISCUITS
5. ASSEMBLIES
6. WRITING FOR NO
   REAL REASON

There's no way, for example, he'd ever read a sentence like 'School uniform takes away people's freedom of expression' and respond with 'Oh yes, I'd never thought of that. Let's scrap it with immediate effect. Thanks for the heads-up.'

Also, on the whole, I honestly don't mind school uniform. I mean, I wish our jumpers were indigo instead of red. And it'd be helpful if any random shoes were allowed (so Mum wouldn't get her knickers (or knockers!) in a twist every morning when we can only find one flip-flop and a hiking boot and we're already running late). But, in reality, if I had to choose a different outfit to wear every school day, there's no way I'd be able to squeeze in five minutes of screen time before our walk to school. I rarely manage it as it is.

TIME TO GO!

So, instead of writing to Mr Epping,
I wrote *my persuasive letter to the rest
of Class Five, outlining the TREMENDOUS
time-saving, screen-extending, decision-
reducing reasons why they should be GRATEFUL
uniform is compulsory at our school.

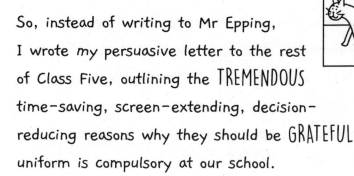

When Mrs Patterson read it, she shook her head.
'You always look at things differently, Billie,' she
said. 'I'm awarding this piece of writing **most
interesting of the day!**'

She also read Janey's letter out. It had no
TEMPTING QUESTIONS or AMAZING ALLITERATION.
In fact, its only interesting part was that, at
her last school, pupils wore slippers indoors. I
will be talking to the school council about that.

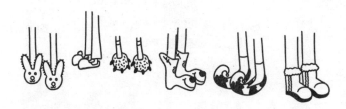

PS Although this diary entry wasn't exactly 'the most MARVELLOUS diary entry I've EVER written' you're allowed to stretch the truth when you're writing persuasively. You're not, however, allowed to outright lie. So please note these two FACTS:

1. I have given the free bag of Haribo mentioned at the start of this chapter to your neighbours. They said they'd keep hold of it until you next go trick or treating.

2. Here is your special voucher. Show it to your teacher to get out of work for a whole morning.

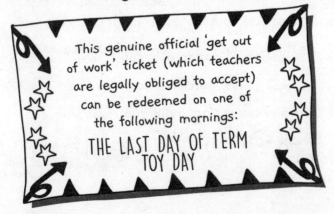

This genuine official 'get out of work' ticket (which teachers are legally obliged to accept) can be redeemed on one of the following mornings:

THE LAST DAY OF TERM
TOY DAY

PRAJIT AND SEEJAY

After dinner today, Mrs Patterson announced some 'important visitors' were coming into class as part of our SPECIAL project's EXTRAORDINARY REWARD.

Now, in the past, announcements like this have led to the arrival of:

1. Mrs Trapp and Mr Ball (our head dinner lady and caretaker, who proceed to inspect everyone's latest work before choosing a 'winner' to write on the dinner-menu board or help mop the hall floor).

2. A selection of random people from Planet OFSTED (who transform our teacher into a calm, encouraging individual who doesn't cancel PE).

3. Someone's granny (who we have to question about the olden days in return for a lecture on how we should take up sewing instead of staring at screens in our spare time).

So imagine our surprise when Mrs Patterson introduced two people wearing fancy trainers and carrying takeout coffee cups. Their names were

Prajit and Seejay, and I knew they were EXTREMELY cool and non-teacher-like as soon as they spoke. Mrs P has NEVER greeted us by saying, 'Hey, guys!'

Anyway, the EXTRA–SPECIAL thing about them was that they work in 'media', making TV adverts and films and stuff. This basically means they're paid ACTUAL MONEY for playing with iPads.

I KNOW! Genuinely interesting.

They gave a talk describing what their
'jobs' involve, then showed us five examples
of adverts they'd made before asking if anyone
wanted to ask a question about marketing.

Thirty arms flew into the air.

Janey asked if they'd ever met
anyone famous. They hadn't
(unless you count an old man our
parents may or may not like to
listen to on the radio — which
we didn't).

Patrick asked how much money
they earned in a year. They
wouldn't say (but I'm guessing
around £6,000,000 based on
their extra-flashy phones).

Elliot asked what type of camera equipment they used. They answered with long words (that only Elliot, who's like an uber-intelligent adult stuck in a kid's body, appeared to understand).

Dale asked if they'd made the FROOT GOOP advert. They said they hadn't (but then found it on YouTube and agreed it was FANTASTIC).

Farida asked if their adverts ever appeared during *Biscuit-Maker* or within any other FABulous games or apps. (Farida, as you may already be aware, grabs any opportunity to use the word 'fab'. Apparently those are her initials. Though so far she's avoided bringing in her birth certificate to prove her middle name's not actually Ingrid.) They said they didn't — and they hadn't even heard of *Biscuit-Maker* . . . SHOCKING!

Layla asked if their adverts were ever on proper telly. They are (but not during kids' shows).

Then I asked what their next project was. This was an EXCELLENT question, as it led to Prajit saying, 'Well, Billie, that leads us **perfectly** on to something exciting we want to discuss with you.'

You'll never guess what ... Film people are FAR more honest than teachers. It **was** something exciting!

PERFECT

'We're looking,' said Prajit, rubbing his hands together, 'for a group of children just like you lot to **star** in a **TV advert** about school uniforms.'

Everyone gasped and started whispering.

The whispers increased to chatter.

The chatter transformed into WHOOPING.

After Mrs P had restored order by playing Copy My Claps as though we were infants, Seejay proceeded to explain more about the advert. 'We're keen to use a good mix of children we can dress in the uniforms for our marketing campaign,' she said.

'And we want to use **normal** kids like you,' added Prajit.

After Prajit had repeated 'YOU'RE ALL NORMAL KIDS, YOU SEE' about thirty-seven times, I decided to mention how Mums say you should never describe people as 'normal' because everyone's normal is different. For example:

1. **My** normal is being the only person in Class Five to own a metal detector, having two secretive and slow-at-organizing-surprise-**FAMILYMOON** mums, and eating chips and eggs for tea.

2. **Dale's** normal is living with his grandad, being a right fidget-bum and climbing anything in sight.

3. **Janey's** is being ~~a pain~~ bendy and having divorced parents.

4. **Layla's** is living in a house full of people who have to use special wide-toothed combs for their amazingly curly black hair (and being a bit obsessed with baby poo).

5. **Patrick's** normal is having hair that never lies down even when you push it, and a mouth big enough to get his whole fist inside.

You get my point, don't you? So did
Prajit, whose cheeks reddened a little
before he explained he meant we were
'ORDINARY' kids, not 'actor' kids.

That made me want to tell him a bunch of
EXTRAordinary facts about Class Five
pupils. Like how Coral Munro can do cool
tricks in her wheelchair. And how
Elliot can spell any word in the
world, even ones with
tricky silent letters
like 'Soon Army'.

(According to my clever friend, this
has a sneaky 'T' in it somewhere.)
I decided not to, though — in case
Prajit decided I was too
UNnormally outspoken to
be in an advert for
school jumpers.

TSOONARMY?
SOONTARMAY?
SUE T NARMY?

Anyway . . . at home time, Mrs Patterson gave everyone a letter so we can chat about the advert with our grown-ups, gain their permission to be filmed and become rich and famous! (Well, famous anyway — I don't know whether we're being paid.) Eek! This is what I call an EXTRAORDINARY treat.

SNIFF!

All the HYPER EXCITEMENT about the school-uniform advert meant everyone (apart from Janey) forgot to bring anything in for TREASURE CLUB today. Fortunately, when I suggested we assemble a gang to play SNIFF instead, Layla and Dale didn't mind a bit (phew) so we've got another week to try to find something better than the 'completely amazing silver horseshoe' Janey said she was DYING to show us . . .

SNIFF is an epic detective game that involves trying to identify the owner of a school jumper within ten seconds using smell alone. I invented it the day after Mrs P lost her rag about people not having name tags in 'every single item of clothing you might ever remove at school' (basically everything except underwear). She'd threatened that NO ONE could go home until the owners of three unclaimed unnamed jumpers were found. Desperate to save everyone from a forced sleepover in a room full of spelling activities, I discovered in a jiffy that each jumper held a unique recognizable smell.

SAUSAGE ROLLY = PATRICK'S

QUITE LEMONY = CORAL'S

A HINT OF BABY WIPE = LAYLA'S

Not only did this solve the mystery,
the next day EVERYONE wanted to see
if they too possessed this amazing power.
That's how SNIFF was born.

We've not played SNIFF for a while but it was
MEGA popular today. Half because everyone in
Class Five is suddenly OBSESSED with anything
school uniformy, and half because Mr Epping had
banned footballs and races.

After we'd created
'Red Mountain' (a pile
of our jumpers on
the playground),
Patrick went first.
Taking a long sniff, he
smirked and declared:

IT'S FARIDA'S. 100%!

'FAB!' said Farida, checking the label to ensure
he was correct — which he was because even
super-pests are good at SNIFF.

Anyway, next Farida sniff-detected Elliot's (metally) jumper. Then Elliot correctly identified Layla's (baby wipes). Layla knew she'd smelled mine (biscuits). I got covered in cuff slime so I knew I'd picked up Patrick's even before I'd sniffed out sausage roll, and then it was Janey's turn . . .

The rest of us instantly knew Janey had picked Dale's jumper (purely based on the streak of whiteboard pen the length of its left sleeve).

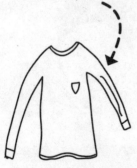

Janey, however, missed this vital (additional and a bit cheaty) clue. She held Dale's sweatshirt as though touching someone else's clothes might POISON her, gave it a tentative sniff, then shrugged her shoulders. When the rest of us had almost finished chanting from ten to one, she mumbled, 'Coral's?'

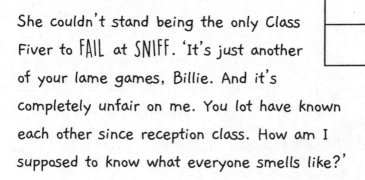

She couldn't stand being the only Class Fiver to FAIL at SNIFF. 'It's just another of your lame games, Billie. And it's completely unfair on me. You lot have known each other since reception class. How am I supposed to know what everyone smells like?'

I suggested she spend more time smelling her classmates and less time doing the splits. This didn't go down well. She chucked Dale's jumper back on to Red Mountain, flung herself into the full splits position and commenced boasting about owning an iPad. 'I video-called my dad last night. He and Benjamin are both so proud I'm going to be a TV star,' she said, smirking at me.

Talk about counting your chickens before they hatch!

'We've not even had our auditions yet, Janey!' said Elliot.

'And you might not get chosen,' I added.

'We'll see,' said Painy, flicking one of her bunches. 'I was first to hand in my permission slip this morning. And Dad's always saying I could be a model or something. Plus, Benjamin's offered to help me if I need any tips. His arms once appeared in an advert about bathroom tiles!'

I decided not to remind Janey about Prajit emphasizing he wanted **normal** kids for the advert (not hair models). Plus, Janey's dad's man friend, Benjamin, didn't strike me as an arm model when I met him. I'm sure she's made that up.

Anyway . . . to increase my chances of
securing a starring role in the advert,
my plan is to practise being 'normal'
when I go TREASURE HUNTING at Gracie Seagull's
this Sunday. (And to find something better than
a horse's shoe.) (And to remind Mum to sign my
permission slip.)

PS Not only is SNIFF a brilliant (and in no way
lame) game, it's also a far quicker and much
more reliable method of finding the rightful
owners of jumpers after PE than searching for
name tags, which nine times out of ten have
either fallen out or faded (or been ripped out
because they said 'BUG' in big black unfadable
marker).

PARTY TIME!

We attended a PARTY at a swanky football club today. We as in my family, not the whole of Class Five. Although a class party on a Sunday sounds like a motion I should be putting forward to the school council who NEVER propose such EPIC ideas.

It was exclusively for families who have adopted children. We've attended loads of these parties over the years. Mums say they're great for helping me realize I'm not the only adopted child in my county. I already know that, of course, but I'd NEVER miss a chance to go to a PARTY.

The best thing about this year's party was befriending a shy little girl whose (obviously awesome) dads were allowing her to play on her iPad while the daft magician did his turn. We hit

it off straight away. As suspected, I am a natural at *Biscuit-Maker*.

The most delicious thing about the party was the chocolate fountain.

Come on, chocolate-chip brownie dipped in melted chocolate — what's not to love?

The most disappointing thing about the party was that, despite my best efforts, I didn't find a single mint hoarder. Hmph.

The worst thing about the party was when a nosy old (mintless) ratbag at the buffet table told me not to take more than my fair share of hot dogs and then insulted me further by thrusting a sheet of paper in my face and saying, 'Would you mind filling in a smiley-face form to say what you think of us holding parties for **kids like you**?'

Grrr . . . I hate it when people lump all adopted children together. Well, apart from when they throw parties for us . . . I mean, could any other kids at the party say they were involved in a hunt for DEAD MAN'S GOLD? Or that they were soon going to be advert-famous? I think not.

THINGS I HATE
7. LUMPING

Well, I gave the old ratbag a piece of my mind, telling her in no uncertain terms what I thought of her phrase choice, then swiped three more hot dogs and took them back to our table. That showed her.

The weirdest thing about this year's party happened at the end. I'd pretty much forgotten about the whole 'kids like you' comment (as you would if you won a bag of jelly babies for claiming victory at Follow-My-Leader Limbo). So imagine my surprise when I returned from my compulsory **'go and try before we leave'** toilet trip only to find old Ratbag herself giving Mums what appeared to be a severe talking-to, no doubt along the lines of **'You'll never guess what your greedy, too-outspoken-for-her-own-good daughter said to me earlier.'**

I was beginning to wish I'd kept my mouth shut and simply taken one of her stupid smiley-face forms, when two strange things happened:

1. Mum S threw her arms round the ratbag and enveloped her in a hug!
2. Mum K began to cry.

I couldn't make any sense of it. Was I in trouble? Was Ratbag trying to steal Mum S from Mum K? Had I entered another dimension in which being told your daughter is a teeny-weeny bit outspoken makes some people extra happy and others mega sad?

'What's going on?' I asked, running to reach for Mum K's hand.

'Hello again!' said Ratbag, releasing herself from Mum S's bear hug. 'I've just been telling your mums how much I admired the way you stuck up for yourself earlier.' (WHAT??) 'I'll be in touch, ladies,' she added, before returning to her precious forms.

Turns out Ratbag (or 'Ruth' as Mums called her) is Wendy's new social worker. (In case you don't already know, Wendy is my birth mother.)

'Is Wendy all right?' I asked, wondering why Mum K still had tears in her eyes.

They said she was fine. I was pleased to hear that as, although Wendy's not my actual mum any more, she did squeeze me out of her front bottom once, so I do care about her.

Despite suspecting Mums were YET AGAIN keeping something from me, I didn't push for more information because Mum K completely distracted me by suddenly offering to download *Biscuit-Maker* on her iPad when we got home!

Biscuit MAKER

LEVEL 10

THE TRIPLE-LAYERED
DOUBLE-DIPPED
CHOCO-CRUMB CREAMY

Now I'm in bed (iPad-less), I can't stop wondering what the huggy-happy-crying-secretiveness was really about.

OMG! Ratbag-Ruth is obviously a **FAMILYMOON** organizer (on her days off from being a social worker) and the reason Mums didn't tell me was because their **BIG ANNOUNCEMENT** is drawing nearer . . . Eek!

I VANT . . . I VANT . . .

We returned to Gracie Seagull's this afternoon. And by 'we' I mean me and Mums, as (boo) they'd again 'forgotten' to ask Gracie about Dale and Layla coming along.

When I saw Gracie in her HUGE yellow wellies and this big grey-and-white mac with sleeves like bat wings, I panicked. Had I missed the fancy-dress instruction for today's hunt? I hadn't. Funny old Gracie just enjoys dressing up like her surname.

I think Gracie must get lonely living in her ENORMOUS house with only her conversation-avoiding dog. 'Darlings!' she shouted, throwing her arms round me before

ushering us into her garden. She'd prepared
perfectly for the continuing ring hunt;
two packets of expensive-looking
biscuits lay on the patio table.

OMG — have you ever eaten a
Viscount? They're UBER-DELICIOUS discs of dark
chocolate and minty cream. Gracie said we could
only have a Viscount if we said, 'I vant . . . I
vant . . . a Viscount!' Apparently this is a line
from a cool-sounding vampire-themed advert
she and early Ronnie used to enjoy millions of
years ago. This rule (which I'm 100% going to
mention to Layla and Dale at our next TOBLA
meeting) was particularly AWESOME; it meant I
got to gobble seven whole Viscounts as Gracie
said one was enough for her, and Mums were too
embarrassed to participate in a little vampire
role play. They didn't seem to mind missing out
TBCH. The fancy Belgian chocolate alternatives
were rule-free. (Though everyone agreed

nibbling the sticky-out edges of chocolate
was the *only* way to start.)
Gracie must have TONS of
money. We NEVER buy such
luxurious biscuits.

Re-enacting the old vampire advert (seven
times) reminded me to tell Gracie my exciting
advert news. 'Oooooh, lovie!' she exclaimed.
'Don't forget me when you're famous, will
you?'

I wasn't aware famous people lost their
memories. Nevertheless, I asked Mum K to take

a photo of me and
Gracie on her phone –
in case my appearance
in Prajit and Seejay's
advert propels me into
some kind of
MEGASTARDOM.

I also asked Gracie if she'd ever tasted FROOT GOOP. She had and guess what else . . .? She knew EVERY WORD of the rap and even performed the ferret's loop-the-loop dance! (Hil.ar.ious.)

Gracie chatted to Mums for a bit after that — mostly about late Ronnie and his 'prize azaleas'. Talking about a bush of pale-pink flowers that once won a Star of the Week certificate didn't interest me in the slightest. So I was glad when Mums disappeared to inspect them, leaving Gracie and me to chat about more interesting topics without interruption.

First we talked a little more about BISCUITS. Gracie said she wasn't the biggest custard cream fan (!) but told me she likes to keep 'abreast' of new developments and would certainly keep her eye out for the chocolate ones next time she went shopping. RESULT!

'To keep abreast of', BTW, is an old-fashioned way of saying 'to keep up with'. As this word is as hilarious as it is drawable, I've decided it deserves a place on both of my current word lists.

HILARIOUS WORDS
1. KNOCKERS
2. ABREAST ⊙

Next we talked about TREASURE CLUB. Gracie said she 'wouldn't mind at all' if I recruited a couple of 'expert jewellery finders' (aka Dale and Layla) to help find the ring if Mums and I didn't succeed today. So I must admit I didn't give DEAD MAN'S GOLD 100% this afternoon. Not solely because of the promise of a TREASURE CLUB expedition and more biscuits, mind you. Gracie also said she wished she had grandchildren of

her own, you see, and I completely understood
her meaning: she wants me to visit more often.
I'm actually thinking of letting her grand-adopt
me. I mean, I know I already have two
grandmas, a grandpa and a great-nan, but the
way I see it you can't have too many biscuit-
buying, new word-teaching, mint-carrying crazy
oldies in your life.

Before we left, I did conduct a cautious scan
around the garden, hoping I might find
something fascinating to present at next week's
TREASURE CLUB meeting. I found:

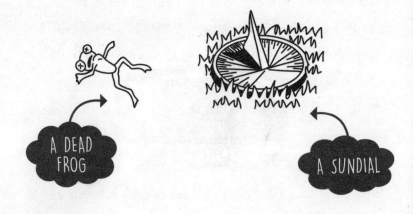

A DEAD FROG

A SUNDIAL

As I'm not convinced the dead frog will be a winner, and the sundial was impossible to pull out from the soil, I'm still on the hunt for something that'll beat Janey's horseshoe on Friday.

On the way home Mums said Gracie's house was so old it might have tons of hidden treasures beneath it. I agreed and mentioned how Gracie had specifically requested I bring backup ring-searchers as a matter of URGENCY. 'Maybe Dale and Layla can come along next weekend?' I suggested, biting my bottom lip. Their responses:

HMPH.

CAGEY

After school today, I was surprised to see Granny Pauline waiting in the yard to pick me up. I'd had no pre-warning about this. Mrs Patterson, however, had. She'd NEVER have let me go home with Granny P otherwise. My school is SUPER-STRICT about teachers not allowing irregular people to collect pupils without prior warning — even if it's someone they 100% know is your granny because they once invited her into class to deliver a talk about sewing . . .

'Hello, you!' said Granny P, gathering me into a perfumey hug. 'Your mums have been held up at work.'

As Mums work in opposite parts of town, and as Granny P was acting as though everything was entirely normal,

I immediately suspected SOMETHING FISHY was
going on. 'What hold-ups exactly?' I asked, my
hands on my hips.

At this, Granny P became extremely CAGEY.
By which I mean she was trying not to tell
me what was going on even
though she definitely knew, not
that she looked like a cage.

'I'm not sure, Billie,' she
mumbled. 'I, err, I think they're
seeing about changing doctors or something.
Come on — let's go and buy you some sweets.'

Nice try, Granny P, nice try . . .

I went along with the sweets bribe (obviously)
but I knew Granny was telling a white lie and
that Mums were CLEARLY attending another of
their SECRET MEETINGS. Besides, there's no way

they're changing doctors. They're constantly telling me how WONDERFUL Dr Pashma is, even though her breath smells of cheese.

A white lie, BTW, is a teeny not-quite-truth, usually told if something secret is going on, or to make sure people's feelings don't get hurt. So when Granny asked me if I'd worn the woolly jumper she'd recently knitted for me, I replied with one of my own before dropping the subject abruptly.

I'M SAVING IT FOR A SPECIAL OCCASION!

The truthful answer to Granny's question, in case you're interested, would have been to tell her the jumper is so ITCHY I will never, ever wear it. It'll go in the white bin bag Mums keep in the utility room and, at some point, be donated to a charity shop. Someone will then buy it for 20p and, when they too discover its itchiness, it'll be thrown in the bin or recycled into a dog blanket or something. Granny P wouldn't have liked hearing this. I just hope we don't have a special occasion to attend together in the next few weeks (unless it involves FAMILYMOON announcements — in which case Granny will be too excited to remember the jumper).

Anyway . . . when Mums finally returned home,
I asked them separately where they'd been.

Mum K said:

JUST FOR A LOVELY
LONG WALK IN THE
COUNTRYSIDE.

Whereas Mum S said:

TO AN
APPOINTMENT.

Over tea, I questioned their conflicting stories.
After a little uncomfortable wriggling, they said
they'd been to an appointment and **then** for a
walk. Nothing about changing doctors at all.

'Was it a SECRET MEETING about your honeymoon?' I asked, finding it impossible to hold my tongue any longer. They said no (hmph) but *still* wouldn't tell me what their TOP-SECRET appointment had been about. I hope neither of them is poorly . . .

Anyway, I told them *I'd* attended a private meeting of my own at lunchtime. This was 100% true. I'd gathered TREASURE CLUB by the big tree to distribute the expedition invitations I'd made while Mrs Patterson had been waffling on AGAIN about the correct way to PEE.

INVITATION

TO_____

FROM_____

P(oint): YOU ARE ONE LUCKY PERSON. →

E(vidence): YOU HAVE BEEN INVITED TO COME ALONG TO SEARCH FOR DEAD MAN'S GOLD WITH ME. →

E(xtra information): NO DOING THE SPLITS PERMITTED. →

CUCUMBER GOOP

All the people who'd brought their slips back auditioned with the filming professionals today, one at a time in the dinner centre. Thankfully, Mum S had left my slip wrapped round my snack. It had a bit of cucumber goop on it, but she'd totally 'signed it'.

I GIVE PERMISSION FOR MY CHILD
Billie Upton Green TO AUDITION FOR THE
FILMING PROJECT AS DESCRIBED ABOVE.

SIGNED:

When it was my turn, Seejay said, 'Hello again, Billie. This is nothing to worry about — we just have to be sure you can follow instructions, and check you're not too shy.'

'No problem!' I said, staring directly into her eyes.

'So, Prajit's going to point the camera at you while we have a little chat, but I don't want you to look at it, OK?'

OMG, have you ever tried following an instruction like that? Hey, YOU! Yes, **you** reading this diary . . . **Don't** look at that BIG SPIDER in the corner of the page . . . about to crawl on to your thumb. ARGH! It's right there! DON'T look! I repeat: DO. NOT. LOOK!

It's so hard, isn't it?

'OK,' I said, trying to avoid glancing at the ENORMOUS camera veering dangerously close to my nose.

'So, Billie,' started Seejay, 'what's your favourite colour?'

I told her it was indigo, which she said she also liked.

'What about food?' she said, her nose wrinkling at the dreadful aroma of steamed cabbage coming from Mrs Trapp's kitchen. 'What do you like to eat?'

I told her I liked biscuits (except Nice ones). It continued like this for a while with dozens of easy questions. Positive I'd secured a place in the advert, my mouth went dry when Seejay studied my permission slip. She didn't accuse me of trying to pass off a blob of squished cucumber as my mum's signature (phew). However, this was the point things started to go downhill . . .

'Oh, how funny,' she laughed. 'Do you realize your initials spell "bug"?'

I gritted my teeth and nodded.

'Remember to speak, Billie —
you're on camera.'

'No one's allowed to call me that unless I give them my permission,' I growled.

'OK . . .?' she mumbled, raising her eyebrows.

'What are *your* initials?' I snapped.

She said they were C. J.

'What are Prajit's?'

Prajit put on a posh accent and said his full name was **P**rajit **O**mar **S**unil **H**amed. Then he giggled (making me suspect this was a COMPLETE LIE and that his name was actually **P**rajit **O**mar **O**akwell).

'Let's move on,' said Seejay (**aka 'CJ'** — doh!), trying to hide her smirk with the fancy scarf draped round her neck. 'Tell us about your favourite book.'

'I like lots of books,' I lied, 'especially ones with hundreds of pages.'

'Wow!' said CJ. 'What are you reading at the moment?'

'Nothing,' I said. 'I'm talking to you.'

CJ laughed (again). 'No, I mean, at home or in class — what's your current book called?'

I wished I'd not 'embellished the truth'. I couldn't recall the name of a single book. 'It's just called Book,' I lied.

Prajit giggled, forcing me to give him a stern glare straight down his camera lens for being rude (and probably lying about his initials).

'Remember not to look at the camera, Billie,' said CJ, before adding, 'I think we'll leave it there.'

So no doubt I won't get a place on the advert and it's all my own fault for getting grumpy about being BUG-ed and pretending to be someone I'm not — an ultra-keen reader of an imaginary book called *Book* . . .

Maybe I'll write it now . . .

Book — a novel by **B**illie ~~Upton Green~~ **O**livia **S**terling-**S**ykes

ONCE THERE WAS A BOOK. IT WAS CALLED BOOK. IT SAT ON A BOOKSHELF FOR BILLIONS OF YEARS AND NO ONE READ IT BECAUSE THEY THOUGHT ITS TITLE SUCKED. THE END.

If I add enough pictures, it'll have hundreds of pages in it, and then I will only be half a liar. You're totally allowed to use a different name from your own when you write a book. (Which I rather wish I'd known before I wrote my first SAD Diary . . .)

THE (NOT ACTUALLY THAT ACCIDENTAL) DIARY OF A BOSS

Janey strutted out of her audition full of it. She said CJ had commented on how much she liked her hair and had asked her to wear it *just like that* for the filming. I SO need to ask Mum to buy me more scrunchies and practise cooler hairstyles. And to stop being a baby about having my hair brushed . . .

OWWWW!

FAMILYMOON

Janey McVey and Farida Banerjee banged on and on **and ON** today about how they're both going to be missing a day of school soon. Farida's getting a Friday off to travel to her cousin's (FABulous) wedding. Janey's having a Monday off to give her more time at her dad's house when she travels 356 miles to visit him and his new(ish) boyfriend, Benjamin (the possible arm model who once called me charming).

All the talk of holidays (and days off school) got me thinking — Bridesmaid Day was yonks ago. What's the big hold-up on ~~Mums' honeymoon~~ our **FAMILYMOON**? So, after tea this evening, when I'd finished work (I detected three pegs, an empty foil crisp packet and 4p) I decided it was high time to suss things out properly.

My timing couldn't have been better. When I

barged into the kitchen, I interrupted something
I suspect was further secret **FAMILYMOON**
planning: Mums huddled in a corner whispering,
one phone between their ears. My arrival brought
the phone call to an abrupt end and, when I
asked who they'd been chatting to, Mum S

blurted out that it had been
'one of those nuisance
call centres'. Now her
usual trick when we receive
post-teatime phone calls
from random salespeople is
to say 'Could you please hold
the line?' before putting the

WE'RE CALLING ABOUT
THE CAR ACCIDENT
YOU WERE NEVER
INVOLVED IN . . .

phone on the table until they've gone away. (Or

SO, YOU LIKE
CHOCOLATE DIGESTIVES,
RIGHT . . .

till I find the phone and
take the opportunity to
widen my **BISCUIT**
SURVEY.) My point being:
I knew for 100% certain
I was being fed YET

ANOTHER lie, so I decided to bite the bullet.
'Are you or are you not planning a term-time
fortnight-in-the-sun-by-a-swimming-pool
FAMILYMOON that you're keeping secret from
me so you can announce it in a posh two-forked
cafe while we eat Eton mess?'

Mums laughed (and pretended not to know what
a **FAMILYMOON** was). When I folded my arms
without smiling, Mum S glanced at Mum K, who
nodded her head and said, 'Billie, you're right
about one thing. There *is* something important
we want to discuss with you. We're —'

And then the phone rang.

It was Layla asking if I'd like to go to her house
for an hour. And, get this, instead of whinging
about homework or saying it was 'far too late'
or 'inconvenient', Mums immediately agreed I
could go. I TOTALLY knew this was to delay

discussing the 'something important' with me. However, I decided being allowed to go to my #BFF's on a school night (and avoid homework) was a reasonable pay-off.

I had lots of fun at Layla's house. Mrs Dixon paid us 50p each to watch baby Neela for half an hour. It wasn't terribly difficult preventing an immobile baby from putting her finger in a plug socket, so essentially we earned 50p each for playing WHAT'S DIFFERENT? and eating biscuits. As you can see, I'm the queen of WHAT'S DIFFERENT?

AMAZING EXAMPLE

LAME EXAMPLE

Now I'm in bed, though, I can't stop wondering what the important thing is. I do my best pondering late at night TBH. OMG, what if they've decided to get a divorce? Before we've even enjoyed a FAMILYMOON . . .

Oh, great, that's all I can think of now. I'm going to have to set my mind at rest. Hang on . . .

SPELLING HOMEWORK . . .

Write sentences to show
you understand the meanings
of this week's spellings.

1. My spellings are
   'ambitious', 'obnoxious',
   'scrumptious' and
   'anxious'.
2. They'd be easier to spell if
   they ended with 'shuss'.

Grrr . . . sorry about that. I should know going downstairs when I'm supposed to be asleep always results in a **'have you learned your spellings?'** conversation. It didn't take long TBCH. I'm better at spellings homework than I give myself credit for — I should probably be more con-she-en-shuss . . .

Plus, it was totally worth it. On my way downstairs I overheard half of a whispered conversation that I'm guessing concerned the 'something important'. Does this, or does this not, sound to you like we're soon going to be embarking on some kind of epic FAMILYMOON camping trip?

MUM K: Are the mini sleeping bags still in the loft?

MUM S: They should be.

MUM K: When shall we tell Billie about the mad option?

MUM S: Soon.

MUM K: How do you think she'll react?

MUM S: She'll be excited. You know Billie. She loves new adventures.

MUM K: Shh. What's that noise?

(GRRR — that creaky stair catches me every time.)

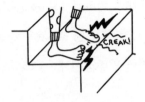

MUM S: Billie! Why are you out of bed?

At that point I pretended I'd just been for my last wee. Well, I didn't want to ruin the surprise completely — or scupper the chances of them holding a posh dinner event where they'll ask for my input about marvellous destinations for tent-based 'mad' **FAMILYMOONS**. (I'm thinking somewhere cool (or hot!) like BARBADOS would be perfect.)

'Well, while you're up,' said Mum K, 'go and fetch the permission slip and letter about that uniform advert.'

(This is the point I wished I'd stayed in bed.)

'Can't it wait?' I fake-yawned. 'I'm so tired.'

They insisted it couldn't — they
needed to check the filming date
was going to be convenient . . .

(This is the point where I wished
I'd not tried to pass off cucumber goop as
Mum's signature.)

'I think I've already handed it in,' I muttered,
hoping our **FAMILYMOON** in BARBADOS wasn't
going to ruin my chances of starring in an advert
about school uniform. 'And I've already
auditioned.'

'That can't be right. We hadn't signed it,' said
Mum S, frowning. 'Go and fetch your book bag
please.'

(This is the point I wished I'd binned the last few weeks' homework sheets instead of stuffing them at the bottom of my book bag . . . although, based on the telling-off I got, the consequences could have been a lot worse than being forced to do spellings.)

Oh well, at least I have a 'mad' trip to BARBADOS to look forward to.

PS I don't remember our sleeping bags being 'mini' . . .

I'M IN!

Morning droning was unusually entertaining today.

First: Mr Epping announced and congratulated the successful advert auditionees. As every single person who auditioned has secured a place, that wasn't totally amazing news. I'm still thrilled, though.

Second: Dale trumped extra loudly!

And third: our head teacher reminded me I haven't viewed any videos of talking animals on YouTube for a while. I'm not sure it was his intention, but it's what I immediately thought of when he shouted at Liam Tabernacle for taking a nap in assembly.

THIS IS WHAT COMES OF BEING ALLOWED TO STAY UP UNTIL THE EARLY HOURS WATCHING VIDEOS ABOUT TALKING DOGS!

Unfortunately, I've still not had a chance to rewatch the hilarious clip of the AMAZING SAUSAGE DOG who can woof 'sausages' while carrying sausages on its head. Layla came for tea tonight, you see, and Mum S BANS screens when I have company. One of her favourite phrases is: **'You can sit there and develop square eyes any other time, Billie; you're not doing it while we have guests over.'** (Which is a lie because I'm currently restricted to two hours of screen time per day whether we have guests over or not.)

Anyway . . . Layla and I sidestepped this INSANE rule by taking turns with my binoculars to watch Mr Greenfield's TV. Mr Greenfield lives

 opposite us and watches cool stuff like cowboy films and *Tipping Point*, which you don't need sound to enjoy. During the advert break we discussed our upcoming filming,

agreeing that, as the only person to write a persuasive letter in *favour* of school uniforms, I deserved the main part.

After tea, we practised the FROOT GOOP lyrics (Layla's almost word-perfect now) and I told Layla more about Gracie's garden before we debated good destinations for camping holidays. Layla suggested Jamaica as she has family there. I told my #BFF that, when the time comes, I'll put her idea forward along with a request that she be my '+1' FAMILYMOON guest. I can't see this being a problem. Mums just love Layla and her 'splendid manners'. Besides, I've heard real honeymoons involve a lot of KISSING, so I'll need someone to keep me occupied when *that's* going on in our three-man tent.

Unfortunately, our chat was rudely interrupted by none other than Janey McVey and her mum knocking at the door. Apparently they'd been having a look round the house that's for sale on my street. Although I was the one who first told Mrs McVey about number twenty-two being for sale, I'm not sure I really want Janey living so close to me. She'd probably badger me to improve my splits every other hour. Also, I wouldn't want Layla to feel left out. She lives a whole ten-minute drive away. Anyway, them bobbing around pretty much ruined the remainder of my and Layla's plans (to continue watching Mr Greenfield's TV).

While Mum told Mrs McVey how super-wonderful living on our street is, I suggested we kids take my metal detector out to the back field to see if we might encounter any more gold-losers. We didn't. We found seven tin cans and Wacky Wanda from up the road searching for her cat's collar.

Although this gave us a proper mission, I was
a bit miffed when Janey located the collar on her
first turn with my metal detector.

Wacky Wanda said she was 'dead
grateful' and told us about how she'd got the cat
in the first place. 'I adopted Jumpy from the
animal shelter about a year ago.'

BEST THING I EVER DID!

When Wacky Wanda had gone,
Janey McVey nudged me. 'That
weird woman's cat's like you, isn't
it, Billie — adopted.'

Layla laughed. I got frustrated. So I told them
both straight: 'The word "adopted" is the only
similarity between me and Wacky Wanda's stupidly
named cat.'

Hang on a sec. There's movement on the landing . . .

VERRUCA

Sorry about that. Mum's just been in. She wasn't terribly interested in looking at my spellings tonight. She just sat on my bed and said, 'Are you OK? You were a bit quiet earlier after Layla and Janey had gone home.'

So I told her what Janey had said and how annoyed I was that she'd compared my lovely family to a crackpot who'd bought a cat with a stupid name.

Mum said, 'Well, I'm with you, Billie. "Jumpy" is a daft name for a cat.' Then she mentioned that Wanda could have changed Jumpy's name if she'd wanted.

That got me thinking about names, wondering if mine had been changed. Had Wendy called me Hoppy or Sleepy or Verruca when I was born?

OH, LOOK AT LITTLE BABY VERRUCA . . .

Mum said she hadn't, then reminded me of the FACTS that I actually already knew: I've always been called Belinda but, when they adopted me, she and Mum K shortened it to Billie and added each of their surnames to make me part of them both. I said I LOVED my name and we had a MASSIVE hug. I didn't mention how I wished Mums had thought about my future life as 'BUG' when they decided to give me two surnames. Could have been worse, I suppose. At least Mum S's surname isn't Mason . . .

SPORK

Janey McVey brought her horseshoe into
TREASURE CLUB today. Although it was the
rustiest object ever, it won because:

A. Dale and Layla both brought in 50p pieces
   minted in our birth year (cool but un-unique)
and
B. Janey managed to convince the others that
   my AMAZING object (a spoon
   that was also a fork)
   wasn't at all special.

'We've got a drawer full of sporks at home!' she
boasted. 'They're as common as butter knives!'

Janey and her mum sure use some fancy cutlery.
I've no idea what a 'butter' knife is either.

Great-Nan's friend Raymond donated the 'spork'

to me after I'd conducted his full-body scan in the special-home's sensory garden the other evening, BTW. I'm not sure why he had tableware in his cardigan pocket instead of mints, but, as he also had a pair of underpants on his head, I swallowed my many questions.

PS I've just overheard a suspicious phone call coming from Mums' bedroom. This time I'm 100% certain it wasn't

a randomer calling about non-existent car accidents as the following statements were crystal clear:

1. We're definitely going to tell her soon and

2. Yes, next Monday at two will be fine.

Something is definitely AFOOT.
My guess is that Mums are
going to collect me from school
early on Monday, whisk
me off to a two-forked
restaurant, and make the
announcement I've been
waiting for! BARBADOS, HERE
I COME!

ANOTHER WORD
THAT CAN EASILY
BE DRAWN!

FILMING

Mums are decorating the spare room. I've no idea why they think our old sewing machine and battered suitcases need a room-makeover, but I wasn't pleased they'd chosen today of all days to start this unnecessary job.

'I thought you said the filming was at one o'clock!' cried Mum S when I pelted upstairs at 9.45 a.m. to chivvy her on.

'This is what comes of us not having the proper information, Billie!' added Mum K.

I'd TOTALLY said 'ten'. They just hadn't been listening. Honestly, their minds are somewhere else at the moment. Even when I showed Mum K a quick YouTube clip about how to do French plaits, she got distracted (by me not having

any shoes on). Then Mum S became all preoccupied about wearing paint-stained clothes (as if the film crew were going to be looking at **her**!). To top it all off, when we (eventually) set off, neither of them managed to focus on Mrs Satnav's instructions.

DO A U-TURN WHERE POSSIBLE.

Consequently I arrived 'on location' for my debut*
filming project half an hour late through no fault
of my own. CJ squinted at her watch and huffed
when we dashed in. I've no idea why (unless it
was because my hair looked like a
haystack) because, OMG, filming an
advert takes FOREVER and there is SO
MUCH hanging around to do — TREASURE
CLUB could totally have had our expedition
to Gracie's garden this morning. Hmph.

Our first 'job' was to sit quietly while CJ
informed our parents what the filming would
involve. When she mentioned the advert was for
A BIG SUPERMARKET, I started to panic. All I
could think about was what Mr 'Precise Uniform
Obsessed' Epping would say if the whole of Class
Five appeared on TV wearing 'non-regulation'
jumpers. Once he got so cross at me for wearing
my 'emergency' supermarket jumper two days on
the run that I offered to draw the school logo on

* This word rhymes with 'grey poo' BTW!

123

it with my whiteboard pen. All I
got for this ingenious idea was
a telling-off for being cheeky.
I still don't know why. Frankly
it's a no-brainer with the
potential to save parents
hundreds of pounds (donatable
to their child's biscuit fund)

I BEG YOUR
PARDON?

because jumpers embroidered with our school
logo cost £14, whereas everyone knows
supermarket jumpers are about 99p. (For obvious
reasons I chose not to air my concerns.)

OH, I SEE. WELL, WE'LL
JUST HAVE TO FIND
ANOTHER CLASS OF PUPILS
TO BE SUPERSTARS.

After that, we had to sit in silence while our
parents signed a bunch of 'release forms'.
(Phew — these were the official 'I agree
100% that my child can appear on TV' ones.)

Once the parents and guardians had left (not before one embarrassing spit-wash incident) there was YET MORE waiting around — this time queuing to be measured by a woman with thick glasses and icy-cold hands. (Brrr.)

Next, guess what! **More** waiting. This time watching Mrs Cold Hands struggle to unpack stacks of boxes filled with our costumes — which she then proceeded to iron!

To be fair, Prajit tried his best to keep us entertained, but his jokes were lame (and no one fancied a bite of CJ's leftover leaf-and-egg sandwich) so our impatience only increased.

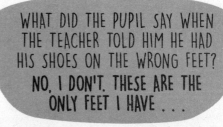

WHAT DID THE PUPIL SAY WHEN THE TEACHER TOLD HIM HE HAD HIS SHOES ON THE WRONG FEET? NO, I DON'T. THESE ARE THE ONLY FEET I HAVE . . .

He didn't even have a hairbrush to lend me.
'The point is that you look like normal kids,
Billie,' he laughed. 'Normal kids don't all have
neat hair.'

Janey's hair looked perfect.
I desperately wanted to pull
one of her ribbons (and
remind Prajit about his use
of 'normal' . . .).

Anyway . . . EVENTUALLY
CJ instructed us to change into the freshly
ironed clothes. I ended up wearing a burgundy
sweatshirt (not great but way better than Dale's
mustard-yellow one; I pity the pupils forced to
wear those every day).

BRB.

SPELLING TRICKS AND TIPS

Spelling	Remembery Method
Uniform	**U**nderwear **N**ot **I**ncluded — **F**ind **O**ther **R**etailer, **M**ate!
Mustard	**M**y **U**ncle's **S**alad **T**astes **A**wesome **R**elish-**D**ipped.
Burgundy	**B**asically **U**gly **R**ed. **G**ood **U**nder **N**avy **D**ungarees. **Y**es?
Purple	**P**atrick's **U**nderpants **R**eally **P**ong — **L**et's **E**xit.
Necessary	**N**ever **E**at **C**J's **E**gg **S**andwiches — **S**melly **A**nd **R**evoltingly **Y**ucky!

Sorry (AGAIN) . . .

Thankfully, spelling tips and tricks are one of Mum S's all-time favourite topics. Not only did my quick-thinking prevent her treating me to a 'it's too late for your light to be on' lecture, it led to her telling me a FUNNY story . . .

When I was in Class One and needed to stay off school (because I had 'the runs') Mum invented a spelling trick to help her learn how to spell DIARRHOEA (which before tonight I honestly thought was spelled diary-a). Listen to this — it's a good one. In fact, I ~~garuntee~~ ~~garantea~~ bet you'll find it useful. (Although writing 'sloppy poo' might still be quicker if you ever have to write a speedy note to tell your parent's boss why your parent took a day off.) Diarrhoea: **D**ash **I**n **A** **R**eal **R**ush! HURRY! (Or Else Accident . . .)

Anyway . . . Once Mrs Cold Hands had adjusted everyone's waistbands to ensure no one's pants fell down, the EXCITING stuff commenced.

First, we played Tig. 'Act normal!' shouted CJ. 'Like you're in your own playground.' That was fun. It was NOTHING like normal, though, because CJ made Patrick be 'it'. (At school

Patrick usually remembers he's desperate for a wee whenever it's his turn to be 'it'. HA!)

Next, we played Peep Behind the Curtain. CJ chose Coral to be on. Coral's so ZIPPY at spinning about in her wheelchair. She got me out every time. Even when I SPRINTED towards her as soon as she turned her back.

After that, CJ put us into groups according to our jumper colour. Our direction was to '*chat without looking into the camera*'. I was in the same group as Elliot and Janey — the burgundies. Elliot said it wouldn't matter what we talked about as Prajit's camera wasn't recording any sound. Nevertheless, I decided to make our 'chat' RIVETING just in case (for once in his life) my brainbox friend was wrong and Prajit was actually listening out for fascinating sound bites to make interrupting TV shows worthwhile.

I kicked off our conversation by describing my metal detector. Elliot had **a lot** of questions.

I wasn't in the mood for explaining technical details in front of Janey so I switched topics slightly. DEAD MAN'S GOLD absorbed Elliot enough that he only glanced in Prajit's camera once (when CJ stood behind him and yelled, **'Remember not to look at the camera!'**).

Janey was BRILLIANT at not looking into the camera. She was DREADFUL at the 'chat'. All she did was neaten her hair and nod her head every time me or Elliot tried to get her to join in.

'Do you like my metal detector, Janey?' Nod.

'Would you like to have another go with it when we go on our trip to Gracie's garden?' Nod.

'Are your ribbons new, Janey?'
Nod, smile.

'Have you noticed the word "burgundies" ends with "undies"?' Nod, slight giggle.

'Can you speak?' Nod. Headshake. Nod.

I think she was a bit nervous. In fact, the only time she stopped nodding was to inform us she's

going on a trip to visit her dad and Benjamin
soon.

'Are you nervous about seeing Benjamin again
now you know he's your dad's boyfriend?' I
asked. Nod.

'Would you like me to come with you, like last
time?' Nod.

This was interesting to hear. I'd love to see
Benjamin again — he's a big sweet-lover like
me. As in he likes eating sweets — I've no idea
what kind of lover he is.

MODEL
ARMS?

After a while, CJ interrupted our chatting so she could record each of us saying a phrase. Janey had to shout: 'Jumping for joy!' Elliot's line was: 'No need to iron.' (An outright LIE, I might add.) I got: 'School uniform needn't cost the earth.' This was a lot to remember on the spot. So I used my bestest LOUDEST voice and changed it slightly.

THIS UNIFORM IS MEGA CHEAP!

I cannot wait to watch (and hear) myself on the finished advert.

When I got home, Mums showed me all the clearing out and painting they'd done in the spare room. I said I hoped the sewing machine liked pale yellow before casually mentioning how much better the room would look with a set of bunk beds. They didn't disagree so I'm hoping I'll soon be able to have Layla, Dale **and** Elliot

for a sleepover at the same time! They'd also cooked 'film-star pie' for tea, so, all in all, it's been a great day. I think I'll leave practising my autograph till tomorrow. Janey has made my brain ache with her constant nodding. I'm exhausted. Oh, look — and I thought my day couldn't get any better!

DRAWABLE
WORD
NUMBER 8!

DOODLE NOTES

Not wanting to admit I'd eavesdropped on their phone call last week, I hadn't mentioned to Mums I knew they were going to collect me early from school today. Attending the arranged two o'clock FAMILYMOON meeting together, however, was on my mind ALL DAY.

In fact, the only lesson I managed to concentrate on was history when I discovered I'd have been the cleverest person in my class if I'd lived in ~~aneshent~~ ~~ainshant~~ old Egypt. Like me, you see, old Egyptians used little doodles to represent words and letters instead of worrying about spellings. Also, they didn't believe in punctuation. How AWESOME is that (I missed the '?' on purpose) (And now the full stop) (And again) (This could go on forever)

Come to think of it, punctuation is a bit boring but it's also maybe a bit necessary sometimes. Example:

NO PUNCTUATION: I like eating cute babies and metal detectors

PUNCTUATION: I like eating, cute babies and metal detectors.

In class Mrs P dished out a sheet of doodles representing the alphabet (she called them ~~hirogliffs~~ ~~hy-ro-glifs~~ hieroglyphs) and gave us half an hour to write our names. It took me less than two minutes to write 'Billie'.

B   I   L   L   I   E

I spent the additional twenty-eight minutes writing notes to Dale using my own (improved) version of hieroglyphs.

At dinner break Layla was so excited to learn our camping-trip announcement was drawing nearer that she drafted a list of what she might bring.

After dinner, I knew I only had a few minutes (aka an hour) to kill before the 'big reveal'. I figured there was NO POINT starting my spellings. Instead I tidied my table and watched Mrs Patterson help Farida and Daisy locate their cardigans (just in the 'check the name tags' way — she never learns).

At 1.45 p.m. I smiled to myself. I'd successfully sidestepped copying out a list of random words declared by Mrs P as essential for all ten-year-olds (but which I seriously doubt I'll ever use, even if I live to be 398).

ME
AGE 398

At 1.55 p.m. I asked to go to the toilet so I could sneakily swing by the office to see if Mums were waiting in a queue to ask Miss Woods to fetch me. (They weren't.)

At 2.10 p.m. I got told off for 'loitering' by Mr Ball who was trying to mop the corridor.

At 2.15 p.m. I got shouted at by Mrs Patterson for staring at the clock instead of writing out my spellings.

At 2.30 p.m. I had to copy the whole ridiculous word list while everyone else got to play outside. (Who uses the words ~~yot~~ ~~yoht~~ yacht and ~~veehickuler~~ ~~veehicular~~ vehicular, BTW? I can't see myself EVER saying, 'Oh, madam, are you bringing your yacht to my super-exciting vehicular party?')

By 3.30 p.m. I was FURIOUS. I'd not been collected from school even ONE SECOND early. My blood boiled further when I marched out to the yard only to find BOTH mums waiting for me — wearing make-up AGAIN.

'Where were you at precisely two o'clock?' I demanded.

Taken aback, they **said** they'd been at home catching up on a few chores. I knew they were fibbing again as soon as we got home: our

breakfast dishes were still on the drainer, the ironing pile remained ceiling height, and the carpets hadn't even been hoovered!

However, as pointing out neglected housework would have undoubtedly led to the interruption of my evening's plans, I chose not to push for the complete truth.

WELL SPOTTED, GRAB
THE HOOVER, BILLIE.

Besides, I still have a vague
hope of being treated to a
slap-up meal in a two-forked
restaurant to be told the 'We're going on a mad
FAMILYMOON to BARBADOS' news. I mean, if it's
not that causing all their secrets and lies, I've
not got a clue what it can be. They'd better not
have been treasure-hunting without me.

OH BOY . . .

A **TOTALLY ANNOYING** thing happened out in the yard today — mainly because Janey McVey has recently become **OBSESSED** with impressing none other than Liam Tabernacle from Class Six. Why, I have no idea. He's the meanest, narrow-mindedest person I've ever met.

'I love the name "Liam", Liam!' she cooed, fluttering her eyelashes in his direction when he got ordered to stand against the wall by Mrs Trapp for kicking Dale in the shin. 'In fact, you know if I'd been born a boy, my mum and dad were going to name me "Liam".'

Liam scowled and stuck out his tongue at Mrs Trapp's back.

'My mum told me I'd have been "Leon",' said Layla.
'But by the time Aaron was born she'd totally gone
off it, so it's a good job I was a girl.'

'I would have been "Meadow"!' added Dale,
rubbing Liam Tabernacle's footprint off
his shin. 'Imagine that.'

'What about you, Billie?' enquired Janey, meanly
asking me something she knew I wouldn't be able
to answer.

I kept quiet. I had no idea what Wendy would
have called me if I'd been a boy. Thankfully, my
#BFF came to my rescue. 'Duh! She'd obviously
have been "Billy", wouldn't she?'

'Oh yeah,' said Janey, shaking her bunches in
Liam's direction and laughing. 'What a SILLY BILLY
I am. You've got one of those weird
interchangeable boy-girl names, haven't you?'

No one else laughed. The whole silly-billy phase was over and done with by the end of Class One. (And, before you ask, Billy No-Mates was old news by the end of Class Four, so don't be childish.)

'Billie's a cool name,' said Dale, giving Janey his best evil eye before turning to me and whispering, 'Better than "Meadow", that's for sure.'

'My girlfriend's called "Charlie",' mumbled Liam, his eyes narrowing and the tips of his ears turning red. 'That can be for boys too, so shut your face, Janey McBobblehead.'

HA! (And double-ha! **As if** Liam Tabernacle has a girlfriend. Charlie's more than likely his dog's name!)

Hang on, Mum's on her way upstairs . . . Apologies in advance — I'm about to start spelling stuff . . .

~~HOMAFONES~~ ~~HOMAPHONES~~
SAME SOUNDS

1. 🐾 v. ▯▯
2. 👀 v. ⎍
3. 🐻 v. 💃
4. 📷 v. 🧍🧍‍♀️
5. 🐰 v. 〰️

Sorry about that. I was right. Mum didn't exactly approve of my Egyptian-based approach to this week's spelling challenge. Her exact words were: 'How is doodling going to improve your spellings? Write the actual words and then turn off your light!'

As she didn't specify **which** words, let me quickly tell you what she said when I asked her if **she** knew what Wendy would have named boy-me: 'I don't honestly know, Billie. But if I ever had a baby boy, I'd call him Felix.'

Ha! Like that's ever going to happen! Unless . . . OMG, I've just had a thought. OMG, Mum's back on the landing. Must dash.

MAILBOX

I've just written my letter to Wendy.
You might not know this, but when you're
adopted you're sometimes allowed to exchange
letters with your birth family once a year. This
is so you can keep up to date with each other.
Because birth parents might not look after you,
but they don't EVER forget about you.

It's a bit of a chore having to write a letter
to someone I don't know, but Mums say Wendy
probably looks forward to my letters so I try
my best.

This year, as well as telling Wendy about my
EXPERT metal-detecting skills and suggesting she
keeps an eye out for a new school-uniform-advert
CELEBRITY, I asked her if she knows what the
appropriate response is when someone hiccups.
Mums aren't remotely interested in helping me

solve this mystery so I figured maybe
my birth mother's bothered about the same
important issues as me.

I didn't forget to ask Wendy my boy name, BTW,
so watch this space. Well, not that one
exactly but you know what I mean. (Although
I'm not sure if Wendy will write back to me.
She sometimes forgets. Maybe Ratbag-Ruth will
remind her?)

PS Mrs Patterson was in a TERRIBLE mood today. It was wet play and not only did she ban everyone from speed-chanting FROOT GOOP, she also refused to let TREASURE CLUB hold a quiet meeting. Semi-disappointed not to be able to share the tinfoil replica of Uranus I'd constructed, I cheered up when Elliot said he'd seen Janey replace a silver charm bracelet in her tray.

HILARIOUS
WORDS
1. KNOCKERS
2. ABREAST
3. URANUS

EXPEDITION

TREASURE CLUB enjoyed a parent-free afternoon in Gracie Seagull's garden today. HURRAY for secret **FAMILYMOON** meetings!

Everyone loved Gracie. Dale and Layla were in stitches when she treated us to an outrageous

FROOT GOOP performance! Janey, who's been in a sulk since no one laughed at her lame 'silly-billy' attention-seeking comment, didn't even whinge when my new old friend produced a bottle of fizzy apple for us to share, even though she once told me she detests anything green. (Which I know for a FACT is a lie.) ------------->

After that, Gracie agreed playing hide-and-seek would be an EXCELLENT warm-up for ring-searching. There are so many AMAZING hiding places in her garden. I wasn't found once; not even when I hid under late Ronnie's lemony-scented prize azaleas with my bottom sticking out — which I honestly forgot Gracie had warned everybody not to go near (the azalea bush, not my bottom).

My seeking skills didn't let me down either. I found Layla hiding under a water fountain, Dale in the upper branches of a prickly tree that smelled of toilet cleaner, and Janey crouched behind a tall stack of mismatched plant pots in late Ronnie's old greenhouse. Although this was a lame hiding place, guess what happened when I tiptoed towards Janey and shouted 'BOO!'?

Answer: she screamed, knocked over the entire tower of pots and cut her knee.

And guess what I heard over Janey's fake-crying?

Answer: a rolling sound.

And guess what I discovered when I went to investigate what exactly had wheeled its way from the stack of pots and straight into Janey's hand?

DEAD MAN'S GOLD!

ON MY VERY FIRST DAY OF SEARCHING AND EVERYTHING!

Typically Janey claimed all the glory. I decided not to argue that I'd heard the rolling first as I didn't want to ruin Gracie's moment. She was so happy she wept the way

adults do sometimes when they're overjoyed.
(Mum S cried at an advert about gravy granules
last night. I didn't know she loved gravy that
much. Imagine how she'll react when she watches
me starring in our school-uniform advert!)

PS Almost better than finding the ring was the
reward Gracie gave us: a packet of THE limited-
edition chocolate custard creams each! OMG,
they were so much better than Bourbons (though
the same TOBLA law applies).

THE CREAM—FILLED COMMANDMENT

THOU SHALT ALWAYS REMOVE THE
TOP LAYER AND SCRAPE OUT
THE CREAM WITH THY TEETH.

PREMIERE

Just before home time today, Mrs Patterson announced that OUR ADVERT was having its first airing on TV between 5 and 8 p.m.

Mum and I IMMEDIATELY decided to hold a RED–CARPET event. We laid a pinkish rug at the front door and, although it was last minute, Granny P, Grandma Jude and Grandpa came round. Granny P even snuck Great-Nan out of her special home and everyone pretended they'd journeyed from far-flung countries to watch a famous celeb starring in a world premiere.

WHO ARE YOU WEARING?

Mum K came home from work early armed with an array of snacks and drinks to accompany the occasion and, at five o'clock, we glued our eyes to the TV.

My heart skipped a beat when the advert came on at 7.15 p.m.

WHAT A DISAPPOINTMENT. I glimpsed my right ear once.

Janey McVey had COMPLETELY HOGGED the screen. It was as though Prajit had been head over heels in love with her ribbons. Her pretty face was shown loads more than anyone else's.

MY RIGHT EAR

There was even a shot of her nodding at Elliot.

Coral was on it a bit, Layla had a close-up, and Dale got his grubby mug on the screen too.

The ending was the worst — a full shot of Janey jumping around all by herself while a voiceover (which, unless they'd used an impressive adultifying voice-changer, certainly wasn't anyone from Class Five) said, 'You'll be jumping for joy with low-cost uniforms that don't need ironing!' (LIES.)

Then some text flashed up:

ONLY £5 FOR EVERYTHING YOU'LL NEED TO KIT OUT YOUR JUMPING BEAN!

(ALSO LIES. Can children attend school without shoes or knickers? No, they can't.)

Stupid.

Stupid.

STUPID.

I told everyone I couldn't believe that, despite being the only Class Fiver openly in favour of school uniforms, I'd been COMPLETELY overshadowed in the stupid advert.

Mums and Granny told me not to be peevish. They said I should be happy for my friends, and pleased my ear had appeared in a professional advert. But I couldn't help feeling miserable. I couldn't even think of a good '**famous body parts**' joke to share with Benjamin the arm model when I go with Janey to see him and her dad.

When Layla phoned, I pretended I'd not had time to sit waiting for an advert to come on TV as I'd been too busy planning my next trip to Gracie's garden and inventing epic games we could play in BARBADOS. 'Oh well,' she replied. 'It wasn't that exciting anyway.' Which I know she said just to be kind. If my face had appeared on telly in the middle of a programme about a vet who can turn three-legged dogs into Olympic tennis champions, I'd have been ECSTATIC.

PS Great-Nan was on my side. She agreed that if Mum had put my hair in bunches, I'd have had a better chance of being the star. Also, she'd brought me a present. It was a toothpick, but it's the thought that counts. My thought being: it could be a handy prodding tool if a CERTAIN SOMEONE gets too BIG-HEADED tomorrow.

KNOT A KNICE DAY

URGH! Today's been one of the WORST days of my ACTUAL life.

In the yard before school the advert was the ONLY topic of conversation. 'It was brilliant, wasn't it, Billie?' gushed Janey, adoring the attention and over-the-top compliments she was getting.

'Was it?' I said. 'I didn't watch it. I was busy playing *Biscuit-Maker*.'

Dale frowned at me while Layla turned towards Coral to compliment her on how pretty she'd looked on TV.

'That old game?' laughed Janey. 'I completed that weeks ago. Hey, El!' she continued, turning her attention to Elliot like he was suddenly her

#BBF. (Hmph — only I call Elliot 'El'.)

DID YOU SEE THE BIT WHEN
I WAS NODDING AT YOU?
IT WAS SO FUNNY!

Grrr. I so wish I'd not encouraged the
burgundies to ask each other a bunch of
nod-worthy questions.

Even Mr Epping seemed OBSESSED by the advert.
Instead of talking about important rules, he
devoted the WHOLE of his precious morning
droning time to showing the juniors the (stupid)
advert and didn't even
shout at Dale for wearing
a non-badged (mustard
yellow) jumper. Then, after
emphasizing how proud he

was of 'the whole of Class Five', he proceeded to single out a few people whose acting he'd particularly admired. Dale and Layla shrugged — like you do if you're proud of something but

don't want to make a big deal of it. But Janey, she grinned from ear to ear and nodded so much her scrunchies nearly fell out. My right ear didn't get a mention.

At morning break Janey's BIG–HEADEDNESS worsened. Producing a pile of scrap paper she'd pilfered from Mrs Patterson's endless supply, she interrupted my and Layla's snack share by inviting my #BFF to go round the playground to see if anyone wanted an autograph.

To be fair, Layla did invite me to join in, but I'm glad I declined. Even listening to Patrick

North boast about his whole arm appearing on telly for two seconds (which even I agreed was more impressive than a millisecond shot of my

ear) was better than watching Janey and Layla thrust scrap-paper signatures on to 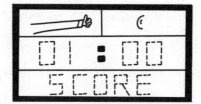 a bunch of unsuspecting infants. RI.DIC.U.LOUS.

As if that wasn't bad enough, after dinner Mrs P cancelled PE in favour of forcing us to spend a whole hour investigating silent Ks. The results of my investigation: they're USELESS. To prove this point I wrote '**Knicola's nickers knever kneighbour her nees**' and spent the rest of the hour illustrating my work. Mrs P said she didn't appreciate my sense of humour. So I said that I didn't appreciate that everyone missed PE just because one person (Patrick) hadn't listened to her '**no talking when you're getting your PE kit on**' instruction.

To top the whole stupid day off, after being made to stay in at afternoon break for answering back, Mrs Patterson put us into twos for history and (probably just to annoy me) partnered Layla with Janey. I got lumbered with Farida who point-blank REFUSED to practise writing notes in hieroglyphs because she wanted to conduct some research about FABulous (boring) old coins.

Who's interested in old coins you can't even spend? NOT ME.

GROUNDED . . .

It gets worse (if you can believe that's possible).

Before I tell you how, let me explain something: being chosen to be register monitor is the best job in the world. (For a Class Fiver that is, not if you're a grown-up. That's got to be being a biscuit tester, surely.)

Why? Well, for one, if you do it PROPERLY (aka saunter to the school office the long way round) you get

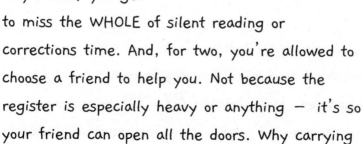

to miss the WHOLE of silent reading or corrections time. And, for two, you're allowed to choose a friend to help you. Not because the register is especially heavy or anything — it's so your friend can open all the doors. Why carrying a sheet of paper and a couple of envelopes would disable anyone's door-opening abilities, I'm not sure. But, as this rule enables friends to catch up on essential gossip, I've never questioned it.

Anyway, now you understand that, I'm positive **you'll** appreciate why I clenched my teeth and slammed my tray shut when Mrs Patterson chose Layla to be today's register monitor and MY #BFF picked Janey to be her helper.

I KNOW! I mean, if not for Layla, I'd still be waiting to discover the joys of register-monitor duties. Mrs Patterson has NOT ONCE decided I'm the actual person sitting the stillest or being the silentest.

At dinner the situation worsened. After harping on about how much fun register-monitor duties had been, Janey invited MY #BFF to accompany her to her dad's for a sleepover next weekend!

'Wait a minute,' I said, my stomach lurching at this terrible announcement. 'You said you wanted **me** to come with you when we were filming the advert.'

'I know,' admitted Janey. 'But Layla missed out last time so I thought it was only fair.'

Although this was true, I suddenly felt eager to limit Janey's #BFF-stealing opportunities. 'Maybe all three of us could go?' I suggested. Layla nodded enthusiastically.

Janey shook her head. 'No, that won't work. Mum's coming down to see some old friends while me and Layla stay with Dad and Benjamin, so we're going by plane. I don't think she can afford a fourth ticket.'

OMG. I've NEVER flown in an aeroplane in my life. EVER.

TIMES I HAVE FLOWN ON A PLANE

PIE CHART

Afternoon lessons gave me zero opportunities to use my AMAZING persuasive skills to change this situation and I ended up having to miss afternoon break to have a one-to-one support session with Mrs Patterson who keeps insisting I'm **still** not PEE-ing properly. GRRR.

WRONG AGAIN

After a pretty sulky walk home, I asked Mum S to come on the trampoline with me. Gentle bum-bounces ALWAYS help when you need to get things off your chest. I told Mum about yesterday's autograph-hunting and this morning's register-monitor tragedy before mentioning the aeroplane-based sleepover I'd been unfairly left out of. Mum put her arms round me and said I should try to feel pleased for Janey getting to see her dad again, and happy for Layla going on a plane trip. 'And anyway,' she added, 'as it happens, you couldn't have accepted even if Janey had invited you because, SURPRISE, we're going camping this weekend!'

This was not the HUGE restaurant-based bog reveal I'd been looking forward to. It did perk me up, though. (As did accidentally writing 'bog' instead of 'big' just then! HA!)

'Where are we going?' I asked.

'Wait and see!' said Mum with a wink.

HILARIOUS WORDS
1. KNOCKERS
2. ABREAST
3. URANUS
4. BOG

SO IT'S DEFINITELY SOMEWHERE LIKE BARBADOS! Which, BTW, will be 100% better than visiting Janey's dad. If *my* trip to see him is anything to go by, that'll just involve excessive sardine-eating and an art-gallery excursion.

(I'm trying to forget about generous Benjamin
and all his sweets.)

That sorted, I left Mum struggling to dismount
the trampoline and hurried inside to watch
Saleema Selective: High-School Detective.
The first half helped me forget about Janey's
annoyingness completely. The advert break,
however, made me throw the controller at the TV.

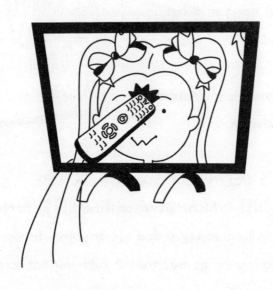

BARBADOS (–1)

Janey and Layla were heading to
the airport straight after school
today. They're probably at Janey's
dad's house now, listening to Benjamin
tell jokes, eating tons of jelly babies
and watching our advert on repeat.

YOUR HAIR LOOKS EVEN BETTER THAN MY ARMS!

They were talking about their plans
ALL DAY. I didn't get involved apart
from to inform them I was off to
BARBADOS to eat mountains of ice cream and laze
by a tropical pool (and to point out there's no
school on Monday so Janey won't be getting the
free day off she boasted about the other week).

It's a shame Mums refused to let me invite
Layla to BARBADOS, but I'm **SO** over Janey not
inviting me to her dad's. Our family-only
FAMILYMOON will be EPIC. Mums were on the

phone a lot this evening — no doubt ensuring our flight is on schedule or arranging last-minute snorkelling adventures — so I've saved them a job by packing my own case.

See you when I get back!

FREE HOT CHOCOLATE

Mums have sent me to bed early to catch up on some sleep because, guess what, I'm back from my **FAMILYMOON**!

Before I go to sleep, I really want to tell you about our AWESOME CARIBBEAN ADVENTURE . . .

Unfortunately, I can't because . . .

~~I'm too tired.~~

We did not go camping in BARBADOS.

Why our **FAMILYMOON** took so long to organize I have no idea as this secret-meetingly arranged trip was at a seaside campsite only an hour from our house, and we didn't even catch a plane to get there. HMPH.

YOU HAVE
ARRIVED.

Also, it rained — A LOT.

I mean, it wasn't **all** bad — especially as Mums
were in particularly generous FAMILYMOON
moods. As soon as we'd pitched the tent, they
took me shopping for a whole new set of clothes!
TOP TIP: totally inappropriate packing has its
advantages (although don't bank on it — you
wouldn't want to be forced to wander around the
Arctic in your swimming trunks . . .). Strangely
in one of the shops Mums kept pointing out tiny
frilly knickers and cute onesies with hundreds of
poppers, asking me what I thought. I said I
thought they were too small. They bought one
anyway and suggested Bramwell
might like to try it. Bramwell
wasn't convinced . . .

After that, they agreed going to
the ARCADES was a much more
appropriate rainy-afternoon activity than a long

wander along the coast. See what I mean about their good moods?! They didn't even complain when I immediately changed the £5 note they'd given me into 2ps and spent an hour trying (failing) to double my money.

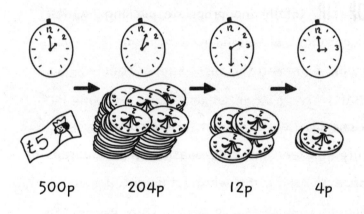

| 500p | 204p | 12p | 4p |

They even splashed out on a fancy meal at a posh seafront restaurant that night **and** let me have my favourite tea — ketchup-covered chips. We only had one fork each, but I didn't mind.

Gobbling our food, we chatted about the awesomeness of their wedding day (aka my Bridesmaid Day) and laughed when we remembered Layla's mum almost giving birth to baby Neela in the middle of the ceremony. This led to a weird conversation during which Mums kept OBSESSING about how super-cute babies are. They weren't particularly impressed when I told them my favourite thing about Neela — that I like it when Layla's mum pays me to babysit her — so I was glad when our puddings arrived. Chatting about babies and what I'd think if one came for a sleepover at our house is impossible when I'm tucking into Eton mess. Besides, our special 'Bridesmaid Day memories' conversation was rapidly deteriorating into a reminder that my #BFF was on a jelly baby-themed sleepover with Painy McVey.

It's possible I overindulged at the restaurant

because, on Saturday night, I was sick all over my (actually normal-sized BTW) sleeping bag. After that, none of us could get back to sleep because the tent REEKED. Every time I almost dropped off, Mums started whispering to each other, so I gave up trying and just lay still, pretending to be asleep in case I heard any private secrets or gossip. I didn't. They mostly whispered about Bramwell's new onesie and whether my old baby clothes were still in our loft. Blimey, I doubt it. A bag of ten-year-old baby clothes sounds like an ideal charity-bag candidate. Anyway, that's one reason I'm so tired now.

On Sunday we managed a bit of crabbing (I caught one crab) and a spot of beach metal-detecting (I found 3p) before the drizzle became hailstones, at which point Mums suggested we go shopping. Now I know shopping during a holiday sounds like the dullest activity ever but, as luck would have it,

on this particular trip, I discovered something
SPECTACULAR . . .

Furniture shops give out
FREE HOT CHOCOLATE!

If you don't believe me, try it for yourself. While
your parents are umm-ing and err-ing over
whether to buy a cot for your sewing machine's
bedroom, explore the shop's ugly-looking but
interesting-to-play-with leather chairs. (And by
'explore' I mean 'mess about with the lying-back
function without removing your shoes'.) When the
salesperson marches over demanding to know
where your parents are, say they're browsing for
items to spend their MILLIONS of spare pounds on.
I guarantee you'll be offered a FREE hot chocolate.

TBCH I was rather disappointed when Mums
ordered a yellow armchair in the fifth such
furniture shop, bringing my hot-chocolate fest
to an early end.

Before returning to the campsite, Mums took me to an upmarket bar. They bought me a mocktail - and we pretended we were in BARBADOS. It was difficult to imagine relaxing in a hammock basking in tropical sunshine while heavy rain pelted

0% ALCOHOLIC

100% SCRUMPTIOUS

against the window and a baby at the next table screamed like Class Two's recorder ensemble, but I appreciated their thoughtfulness. I didn't even mind them banging on about babies again (although it was annoying that they were more interested in telling me the screamer's high-chair was exactly like the one I used to have than listening to my request that we move to the 'no under-threes' area of the bar).

Anyway, I climbed in to my sleeping bag on Sunday night feeling much better about missing Janey's sleepover trip (and a bit sick).

Unfortunately, during the night, the wind turned into a FULL—BLOWN THUNDERSTORM. So much so that by the early hours of the morning our tent had ripped away from its pegs. Standing in the middle of a field in our pyjamas, clinging on to the tent canvas for dear life wasn't an ideal end to our FAMILYMOON but by that point Mum K said she'd HAD ENOUGH. That's the other reason I'm in bed so early.

PS Although I'm not sure I'm comfortable classing this semi-disastrous trip as our **FAMILYMOON**, at least all the SECRET MEETINGS and suspicious phone calls will now stop.

PPS If I fall asleep in class tomorrow, shall I fake jet lag?

GRACIE—OUS ME!

Guess which of these EXTRAORDINARY things happened today?

A. Dale said the sound 'th'.
B. Janey wore a plain elastic bobble.
C. Layla announced her mum is pregnant AGAIN.
D. I found some ACTUAL treasure in Gracie Seagull's garden.

The answer is . . .

ALL OF THEM!

Well, except C. Wow, Layla would be FUMING if that happened. The Dixons have so many children now she's been banned from getting any new shoes until her old ones have 'fallen off her feet'. (Another reason I'm happy to be an only child TBH. I might have had to plod around the puddles of Rainsville in my flip-flops if Mums had had more than one child to re-wardrobe on FAMILYMOON.)

Anyway . . . what a day. I mean, look at B! And A! I thought Dale was going to say 'fank you' and 'frew' his whole life.

D is the OMG-est, though. Listen to this . . .

Mum dropped me off at Gracie's after school today so I could give her the low-down on our FAMILYMOON. There's only so long you can talk

about free hot chocolate, vomit and tent disasters —
so I'm glad I took along my metal detector.

Anyway, after we'd finished our refreshments
(fizzy orange and Wagon Wheels today) Gracie
went to wash up, leaving me to conduct a
tentative scan for more lost jewellery. My metal
detector went BONKERS when I popped it under
late Ronnie's azaleas so, uber carefully, I dug up
a small section of soil.

When I spotted a 2p-sized filthy disc, I hoped
I'd found a mud-preserved Quality Street toffee.
I was a tad disappointed when I gouged
off the dirt and discovered it was just
an old coin.

When I showed it to Gracie, two things happened:

1. She **oohed** and **aahed** A LOT.
2. She **oh no, oh deared** a bit (when she discovered where I'd found it).

Anyway . . . after I'd refilled the hole, Gracie suggested we take the coin to the museum in town. I'm not overly keen on our local museum. It's not one of those ones where they let you touch stuff. But catching a bus sounded fun, so I called Mum to ask for permission and off we set.

By the time we arrived at the museum and the old coin expert had been located, it was nearing half past five. (And by 'old coin expert' I mean she was an expert in old coins. I'm not sure of her age.) Her name was Dorothy McCorkingdale and the first thing she did was look at her watch and huff. I'm so glad Mrs Patterson forced us to do all that work on persuasive techniques — it only took me twenty-four seconds to convince her to stop whinging and start inspecting our coin.

THIS COIN COMES WITH A FREE BAG OF HARIBO . . .

Pulling a weird magnifying glass from behind her ear, her eyes lit up.

To cut a long (and a bit dull in parts if I'm honest) story short, according to Dorothy McCorkingdale, my coin looks '**remarkably like a penny from the thirteenth century!**' That's an EPICALLY long time ago — YONKS before even Great-Nan had been invented.

'Eight hundred years ago!' exclaimed Gracie. 'Goodness me! Isn't that when Edward the First was king?'

Dorothy McCorkingdale praised Gracie for her random (but impressive) knowledge of royalty then informed me Edward the First had dark curly hair, a droopy eyelid, spoke with a lisp and was also known as 'long-legs'.

'Did he have any children?' I asked.

Dorothy said he had SIXTEEN, so if he's not the reason why we call crane flies daddy-long-legs, he should be.

'If I'm right,' said Dorothy McCorkingdale, turning my coin between her fingers, 'this could be classed as quite a special find, young lady.'

I nodded politely, assuming Dorothy was about to treat me like a baby and call one old coin buried in a garden 'treasure', when . . .

SHE DID!

But she wasn't treating me like a baby. She was being GENUINELY HISTORICAL. According to Dorothy, if you unearth a coin that's proved to be more than 300 years old and made of over 10% precious metal, you're entitled to call it treasure! Although she said she couldn't be certain, she's going to get my coin tested and,

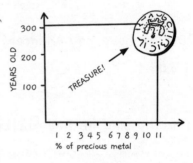

chances are, I will be known as an OFFICIAL TREASURE-FINDER.

Layla and Dale are going to be GOBSMACKED. Maybe my news will even shut Janey up. Honestly if she tells me one more time that Benjamin took her and Layla waterskiing **and** kayaking, I might SCREAM.

HUGE BRA

I found a HUGE bra on our garden fence this morning. As last night was particularly windy, I'm presuming it belongs to Shirley from next door (or Stan — you never know) and had blown off her washing line. Because I wasn't sure, and as I didn't fancy conducting an extended door-to-door investigation, I presented it at TREASURE CLUB today.

Dale said it was the BIGGEST BRA he'd ever seen before suggesting it could be used as hats for twin babies. We laughed so much that I WON the champion-finder title!!!

(Telling everyone about my ancient-coin find helped too, I think.)

I DARE YOU TO WEAR IT AT HOME TIME!

Something even better than winning TREASURE
CLUB happened after school when I found Gracie
in the yard with Mum. She gave me a big hug,
asked me why I had a bra on my head, then told
me she had exciting news.

'Dorothy McCorkingdale's been in touch,' she
said, her eyes twinkling. 'The coin experts have
inspected our coin.'

GUESS WHAT?

It's OFFICIAL — our coin is 100% TREASURE and I can now call myself an ACTUAL TREASURE-FINDER. Can you believe it?!

Even better — Gracie had baked chocolate shortbread biscuits to celebrate this news. She'd wrapped them in gold foil so they resembled chocolate coins and she called them 'pieces of eight'. I'm not sure why she didn't just call them 'zeroes', but I didn't say so because they tasted **almost** as epic as Jaffa Cakes. FACT.

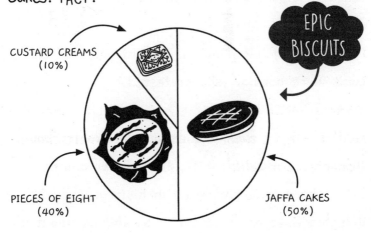

CUSTARD CREAMS
(10%)

EPIC BISCUITS

PIECES OF EIGHT
(40%)

JAFFA CAKES
(50%)

TURBO WRITER

Some people almost fainted in amazement hearing about my ACTUAL TREASURE find during ~~show and~~ tell today. Mrs Patterson even requested an EXTRAORDINARY assembly so I could talk to the whole school about it.

Mr Epping was INSANELY impressed. 'Old coins are fascinating, children,' he declared.

I agreed they were fabulous and then Mr Epping asked if anyone had any questions.

Farida raised her hand. 'I thought you said old coins were boring,' she protested.

As this wasn't even a question, I told Mr Epping that Farida must be mistaking me for another Billie she'd once partnered in history. Then I diverted everyone's attention by talking about my

metal detector and Edward the daddy-long-legs
and his sixteen children. (It worked.)

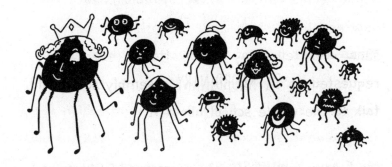

After school, even more excitement! I went to
Gracie's house to join her (and Dorothy
McCorkingdale) in an INTERVIEW for our local
newspaper about our treasure find.

The newspaper reporter asked me loads of
questions and filled two full pages with notes
about TOBLA, TREASURE CLUB,
my metal detector and my
discovery of late Ronnie's ring
before I'd even mentioned
the buried coin.

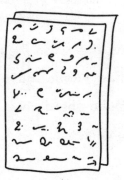

She also snapped a photo of the three of us beside late Ronnie's prize azaleas and told us the article will be in tomorrow's paper. I can't wait!

When Mums arrived to collect me, they looked like they'd travelled via Custardville. Honestly the spare room's getting A LOT of attention at the moment. As well as pale-yellow walls, Mums have now painted its wardrobe bright yellow, given it our new yellow armchair and fitted a lampshade covered with cute little sunshines. That's one lucky sewing machine.

IN THE NEWS

As soon as we could, we bought a newspaper today. I'm guessing the reporter lost the notes she turbo-scribbled about me; her article was rather brief. Look:

Gracie Seagull (72) of Ribchester Avenue got more than she bargained for when she enlisted local schoolgirl Billie Upton Green to help her locate her late husband's wedding ring. Buried beneath an azalea bush, a coin was discovered by the youngster, and has been confirmed by museum curator Dorothy McCorkingdale as a silver penny dating back to the 1200s.

Declaring the find as 'treasure', Ms McCorkingdale added, 'Depending on their condition, coins like this can fetch more than £90 when sold.'

Mrs Seagull said she has no interest in selling the coin, but will allow the council to do a 'careful dig' on her property, which museum staff suspect is built on a medieval settlement. 'As long as my late husband's prize azaleas are not destroyed!' she added.

Although it didn't mention TOBLA or TREASURE CLUB or any of the 'prize-winning' details Gracie had shared about late Ronnie's azaleas, it did lead to something INSANELY EXCITING . . .

A phone call! (Not a secret one, thank goodness — I so don't miss those.) It was from a woman who puts things together for the local TV news. She asked Mum if I'd be available to go to their TV studio to help Gracie do an ACTUAL TELEVISION INTERVIEW!

ERR, YES!

I rang Gracie straight away. **Her** main concern was what she might wear. I suggested her seagull outfit. She said she'd only wear it if I dressed as a bug, so we're just going to decide on the day.

PS IN YOUR FACE, non-badged uniform advert

makers!! I'm 100% going to be more famous than Janey McVey and her scrunchies. Better practise my signature in case everyone who watches demands an autograph!

ON THE ACTUAL NEWS

Nothing special to report.

JOKES!

I was on the news today! THE ACTUAL NEWS! On television! LIVE!

OMG. It was WAAAAAAAAAAAAAAAAY better than ~~starring in~~ nodding my head in a TV advert without even speaking.

V.

First the news lady asked me how I felt about finding treasure. I said, 'I'm pleased because nearly ruining Gracie's dead husband's prize azaleas was worth it. She's not as cross with me now she knows what they were hiding.'

The lady laughed and asked me if I felt like a pirate.

I frowned. 'No, I'm not a baby. I feel like an architect.'

'Don't you mean an ~~arkeeolajist~~ ~~arceeologist~~ archaeologist?' she said, trying not to smile.

I said, 'Yes . . .'

Then she spoke to Gracie. Gracie used her poshest, BOOMIEST voice and kept repeating how astonished she was that bumping into me by a poo bin had led to her appearing on the news (and talking about Ronnie's azaleas).

When it was Dorothy McCorkingdale's turn to answer questions, she droned on about history for AGES.

The only thought-provoking thing she said was that a team of experts with 'special tools' will soon be starting their 'dig' to check if Gracie's garden is hiding anything else of historical significance. No doubt they'll appreciate some help from me and my awesome metal detector.

Before the interview finished, the news lady asked me if I wanted to say anything else.

Dorothy had pretty much exhausted the coin find by this point, so I took the opportunity to address another important issue. 'Hello, prime minister,' I said, staring straight into the camera (100% allowed today). 'If you're watching, please could you get back to me about the Biscuit Laws?'

This was a great thing to say — it majorly livened things up after Dorothy McCorkingdale's history lesson. Keen to hear the full details of all TOBLA's Biscuit Laws, the news lady's forehead crinkled when I told her that Layla and I haven't received any replies to the twenty-six letters we've sent to 10 Downing Street.

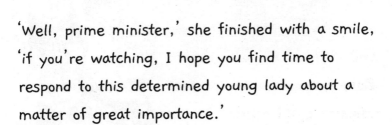

'Well, prime minister,' she finished with a smile, 'if you're watching, I hope you find time to respond to this determined young lady about a matter of great importance.'

All the adults laughed. I remained serious and gave the cameraman my best slow-blink. Biscuit Laws are no laughing matter.

Appearing on TV wasn't even the best part of this AMAZING evening. GET THIS! When we were ushered into the green room (which is what the TV people called their waiting room — but that was not 'green' in any way) guess who we found watching the news on a big screen . . .

ZAKK-O!

In case you don't know, he's Layla and my all-time favourite celeb. He stood up, ruffled my hair with HIS BARE HAND and said he liked the way I'd put a question to the prime minister on live TV!

Completely STAR-STRUCK, I just managed to ask him what his favourite biscuits were (pink wafers — yum!) before he exited the non-green room and headed towards the news studio.

Driving home, Gracie said I'd always be her favourite ~~architect~~ archaeologist and persuaded Mum to stop at a petrol station so she could treat me to some pink wafers. Unfortunately, she returned to the car with an air freshener and the only packet of biscuits they had in stock, but that didn't stop today being one of the most AWESOME experiences of my life.

GINGER NUTS

BLEURGH!

Billie-O
B.U.Green
B-Green
B.U.Green
Billie U Green
Billie Upton Green
Billie Upton Green
Billie Upton Green

AUTOGRAPH

At school absolutely EVERYONE (except a lot of people) wanted my autograph, so I'm glad I'd perfected my signature. I mean, I was NOTHING like Janey had been after the lame uniform advert. I didn't FORCE myself on to the infants or get so big-headed I couldn't fit through the classroom door or anything. I merely obliged when people requested one, and answered politely when they asked if I'd met anyone famous.

WHAT DO YOU MEAN, 'WHO'S ZAKK-O?!?!

Layla told me NEVER to wash my hair again. I'm considering it, but since Dale squeezed his cherry-tomato juice all over it at break time,

I might not have an option.

Janey said her mum had been enjoying *Eggheads* so she hadn't watched the news (as if). Luckily Mrs P found it on the internet, which meant that the whole class got to enjoy my fame together.

'Well, how fascinating, Billie,' said Mrs Patterson when she paused the clip (before Zakk-O's interview about his upcoming concert sadly). 'Does anyone have any comments or questions?'

Coral said she liked my tights. (I said thanks.)

Dale commented on how weird my voice sounded on TV. (I agreed.)

Patrick asked me why I hadn't brushed my hair. (I chose to ignore him.)

Farida said she thought the interview was
FABulous. (I didn't even roll my eyes.)

Elliot said I was his hero (and taught
Mrs Patterson how to
spell 'archaeologist').

But, most surprisingly,
guess what Janey McVey
said?

She told me I was the most famous person she'd
ever met! (I said thank you and
immediately felt a bit guilty for not
supporting her advert fame better.)
Maybe I'll offer her a small
behind-the-scenes role in the big-
budget TV show I'm going to ask
Prajit and CJ if they'd be interested in
producing with me?

PS Mums have finally finished decorating the sewing machine's bedroom. It's ever so pretty now it's carpeted, and Grandma Jude's home-made 'starry night' curtains are hanging at the window. You know what? Although it's smaller than mine, I'm seriously considering asking if I can swap rooms. Or, better still, maybe I could have TWO ROOMS. Then I'd be like Janey. She's always going on about having a second bedroom at her dad's.

JAMMIE DODGERS

An official-looking creamy-coloured envelope was waiting on the kitchen table for me after school today. I rarely receive letters through the post, so my excitement levels were high even before I ripped it open and discovered who it was from. You'll absolutely NEVER GUESS (unless you lower your eyes one centimetre, in which case that's cheating, not guessing) . . .

THE ACTUAL PRIME MINISTER!

Get a load of this . . .

OM ACTUAL G!

10 DOWNING STREET
LONDON SW1A 2AA

Dear Billie,

Thank you for your recent letters, which I very much enjoyed reading. Please accept my sincere apologies for the delay in my response, but I hope you might agree when I say better late than never.

Although I personally agree with you and your friend Layla on the very serious matter of how biscuits should be devoured, I'm afraid I cannot make laws to enforce such rules. Might I suggest, however, an additional rule for TOBLA to consider? It's one I've been known to employ when the greedier of our world leaders come to 10 Downing Street:

The 'Hide Them and Hope' Amendment — when supplying a plate of biscuits for meetings, one must try one's best to conceal the tastier biscuits beneath a mountain of dreadfully dull shortbread fingers so one can gobble them in peace when one's guests have departed.

With kindest regards,
The prime minister

PS My favourite biscuits are Jammie Dodgers.

I will be writing back ASAP. We could become actual pen pals. Blimey, I could have a guest slot on **Treasure Hunt With Billie** for all my famous friends!

P.M.	
Z-O	
B.U.G.	

FAMOUS PEOPLE'S
FAVOURITE
BISCUITS

BISCUIT MORNING

Layla and I shared our letter from the prime minister at show-and-tell today.

Mrs P was the most impressed. She literally squealed when she realized she and the prime minister share a love of Jammie Dodgers. This surprised me TBH — I'd always thought of my teacher as more of a boring old rich-tea candidate. (Her squeak was a surprise too.) In her giddiness she allowed us to chat about our favourite biscuits for five whole minutes and even let us play biscuit-themed hangman instead of doing spellings! No one got mine . . .

p i e c e _
  o _
e i _ _ t

I felt mighty pleased with myself until Patrick

North 'bugged' me. 'That letter's a fake,' he whispered. 'Just like your bogus biscuit. There's no way the actual prime minister would have written to a bug like you.'

I knew Patrick's moodiness was because I'd beaten him at his favourite game. Nevertheless, I told him that if he brought back the whole **'calling me Bug'** thing, I'd tell Mrs Patterson he'd copied all his PEE comments off Elliot for the past fortnight. That shut him up (so it was a decent guess).

After school, though, I considered what my annoying 'friend' had said, and my mind immediately wandered to Great-Nan. I wouldn't put it past her to pinch stationery from the government to make me feel good. To conduct a sternly questioned interview I suggested a post-teatime trip to the special home.

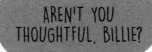

AREN'T YOU THOUGHTFUL, BILLIE?

I don't believe Great-Nan sent it — when I asked her to show me the computer she uses to type letters, she took me to the home's kitchen and pointed at the toaster . . .

PS While we were at the nursing home, barmy Raymond told me he'd seen me on the news and asked me to autograph his Zimmer frame. I did — with a bright-pink lipstick he produced from his waistcoat pocket. I like Raymond a lot. (I think Great-Nan does too!)

#BFF (+1)

Before school today Mums said they had an appointment at 4 p.m. 'You can come if you like, but Layla's mum's offered to take you to Victoria Park instead if you'd rather.'

Bit of a no-brainer really, especially since SECRET MEETINGS are a thing of the past. I darted away to call my #BFF but the spring in my step diminished when I learned Janey was coming too . . .

Victoria Park is usually epic. Tonight it was so-so. 'So-so' is a word Granny P uses a lot. It means 'OK but not great'.

ANOTHER DRAWABLE WORD!

For one, it was spitting so the mini train wasn't running.

For two, the drummer performing in the bandstand wouldn't let us have a go on his kit.

For three, we spent a lot of time waiting outside the boys' toilets as Layla's three brothers are completely unable to hold their FROOT GOOP and

Mrs Dixon refused to let them pee behind a tree. And, for four, we encountered Liam Tabernacle's extra-mean ~~girl~~bullyfriend, Charlie, in the giant basket-swing queue.

'Look who it is!' she said, nudging Liam in his ribs. 'That girl with two mums from your school who found some old stuff in a weird old woman's garden!' Jabbing her finger towards me, she added, 'All our school had to watch you on the news.'

Although hearing that other schools had watched me on TV made my eyebrows shoot to my fringe, I could tell this Charlie girl wasn't being particularly complimentary. 'For your information,' I said, 'Gracie Seagull is not weird.'

'You're weird having two mums,' shouted Charlie, turning to Liam and laughing.

A large lump immediately formed in my throat preventing me from giving a smart reply. Thankfully, my two best friends had my back. This is the point I remembered how AMAZING

Janey is (when she's not being a wannabe).

'Having two mums isn't weird,' said Janey, standing face to face with the bully. 'Accosting someone you don't know and criticizing them is, though. Are you so insecure that you need to pick on other people just to make yourself feel good?'

'Who asked you, Bobbles?' she shouted, her face flushing.

'I asked her!' lied Layla, stepping in front of Janey. 'You just didn't hear me because you were talking so much in your loud annoying voice.'

The bully might have been mean, but she wasn't terribly clever. All she said to that was: 'Come on, Liam. Let's go to the ice-cream van — I've had enough of these weirdos.'

Liam scuttled after her, but I noticed he turned round with a kind of apologetic face. I felt sorry for him. He could do better. Like me — I'm so lucky having friends I'm not scared of like Layla and Janey.

'Seems like you're miles more famous than me now, Billie,' said Janey as we headed to the car park. 'Being on the news for something interesting is tons better than appearing in an advert about boring old school uniforms.'

'I don't think so,' I said truthfully (and seriously rethinking my desire to be prime-time TV-famous — who wants to be accosted by rude randomers in the queue for the basket swing?). 'Your advert is on practically every day. You can only watch my interview now if you search for it online.' (Which I do — a lot!)

Janey shrugged. 'Are you OK?' she asked, reaching for the hand Layla wasn't already holding.

'Thanks for sticking up for me, guys,' I said, throwing my arms round Janey. 'I promise I'll always do the same for you.'

And I will — 100%. Janey's my #VBF after all.

PS Right now I'm more than happy to let VB stand for VERY BEST. In fact, I've not seen Janey do the splits once this week.

PPS On our way home Neela giggled and gurgled

so cutely at my funny faces and crazy noises I began to wish I had a baby sister — till she let off the SMELLIEST trump I've ever had the misfortune to be trapped in a car with (and then

BOPPED me on the nose with her solid rubber giraffe).

PPPS I didn't mention to Mums what Liam's bullyfriend had said. Instead I asked if they'd buy me a drum kit as well as some bunk beds for the yellow room.

Their answer: 'It's late. Can we talk about this tomorrow?'

NO MORE SECRETS!

You **WILL NOT BELIEVE** what Mums have just announced . . .

We'd just finished watching an inspiring programme about a girl with one leg who'd climbed an enormous mountain, when they started a conversation about hopes and dreams and things **we** might like to achieve.

Brimming with ideas, I listed my top three:

1. Become a professional drummer.
2. Convince my new pen pal to consider publishing my dictionary.
3. Contact more local oldies to offer my garden-scanning services.

DIC-SHUNN-ARY

WORDS MUST ALL NOW BE DRAWN (OR SPELLED EGGZACLY THE WAY THEY SOWND)

BUG

Mums glanced at each other, held hands and said they had some EXCITING news that would help fulfil one of **their** dreams.

I hoped they were about to tell me they'd organized a WONDERFUL fortnight-in-the-sun-by-a-pool holiday for our PROPER **FAMILYMOON**, or that Zakk-O had sent us free tickets for his upcoming concert.

But, guess what, it was FAR MORE exciting than anything on my list . . .

WHAT WOULD I THINK ABOUT HAVING A BABY SISTER? they asked!!!

Turns out my birth mother, Wendy, had a baby a few weeks ago and she asked her social worker (Ratbag-Ruth) if Mums would consider adopting her so she can be part of OUR WONDERFUL FAMILY.

Mums said they'd been told a while ago Wendy was expecting another baby, so they'd thought about it a lot during the past few weeks. Then, once the baby arrived, they'd attended a few meetings. (DON'T I KNOW IT! I did think our seaside camping trip was a bit lame to have involved so many hush-hush conversations, random phone calls and teary hugs — OMG, I've literally just realized . . . 'm**AD OPTION**', '**MINI** sleeping bags' . . . how could I have been so dumb?)

They PROMISED me they've not seen the baby yet, and semi-apologized for keeping secrets by explaining they'd wanted to explore all the '*ins and outs*' and '**be sure it was really going to happen**' before getting me too excited (AS IF!!!!).

We had a HUGE family hug and I told Mums I forgave them for the SECRET MEETINGS and said I thought it would be AMAZING to have a baby sister. After a few happy tears, Mums said an adoption expert wants to come and talk to **ME** to hear my true thoughts and feelings.

I know I will have a lot to say!

OMG —I'm going to be a role model.

OMG —I might have to use the baby-poop
      categorizer me and Layla invented.

OMG —I hope the baby likes yellow (and sharing
      her room with a sewing machine).

OMG —I feel another (un)SAD Diary
      coming on . . .

MUM!
I NEED
ANOTHER
SPELLINGS
JOTTER!

PS I can finally **PEE** properly!

P(oint):   I am the queen of fast rapping.

E(vidence):   I know this because I can say
                  every word of FROOT GOOP
                  perfectly in twenty-nine seconds,
                  which is one second faster than
                  anyone else in my class.

E(xplanation):This shows me that I will be
                  AWESOME when it comes to
                  teaching my new baby sister
                  ESSENTIAL life skills.

Catch up soon?
Billie X

A NOTE FROM PUFFIN

Wondering what to read next?

P(oint): You should read *The Accidental Diary of B.U.G: Showstopper.*

E(vidence): We know this because we've had a sneak peek at it and it's completely awesome.

E(xplanation): This shows that us that people like you will definitely want to get stuck in as soon as it's out (JANUARY 2022, BTW).

ACKNOWLEDGEMENTS
(AKA THE BISCUIT AWARD
CEREMONY OF THANK YOUS)

INSTRUCTIONS: Imagine you're at a school awards ceremony. Sit back, half wonder whether you'll get a mention, and save your applause until the end.

JEN: Is this mike on? Good. Ahem . . . Thank you so much for being here on this ~~orspishuss~~ ~~auspitious~~ positively wonderful occasion. I'm honestly delighted to have been given this chance to publicly air my gratitude to a few of the people who got me to this point, because — although I might have written the words and doodled all the pictures — bringing a book to market involves a HUGE amount of teamwork.

First off, a huge thank you to my agent, CHLOE SEAGER, from the Madeleine Milburn Literary, TV and Film Agency. Chloe's probably similar to your #BFF. As well as being a wonderful, funny and encouraging person, she told lots of publishers that my books were amazing, even though she's unrelated to me. Chloe — you rock and you are duly awarded a JAFFA CAKE.

Second up, thank you to the whole team at Puffin who not only made me feel like the actual queen when I went to visit them in London in 2019 but have been working tirelessly to make my BUG books shine since then. There are a gazillion people at Puffin and oodles of them have helped to get this book into your hands, but, in particular, I'd like to give an extra-special mention to:

a. EMMA JONES — my clever and insightful editor extraordinaire. Emma's like that teacher you wish you could have forever. They might tell you to try harder sometimes, but you know you'd be lost without them. Emma, I can't thank you enough.

b. WENDY SHAKESPEARE — my managing editor. Wendy's probably related to William she's THAT good at grammar and punctuation. Wendy, it's an absolute pleasure laughing with you and learning from you.

c. EMILY SMYTH — my design manager. Emily is the creative genius who, among other things, designed the fabulous covers for my books, which I think are fantabulous. Thank you so much, Emily.

d. HARRIET VENN and JANNINE SAUNDERS — they're responsible for all the superb promotion my books have had. They're like the human equivalents of your school website, keeping everyone informed and trying to get everyone to join the netball team. Thank you, guys!

It's CHOCOLATE DIGESTIVES all round for #TeamPuffin.

Moving on, my third thank you goes to JANENE SPENCER. She's the clever designer who puts everything together on the pages before they go to print. I'd compare Janene to the teaching assistant who actually does all the hard work to make your corridors and classrooms look snazzy. I hereby award Janene with a HOME-MADE GINGERBREAD PERSON WEARING A FUNKY DRESS.

Fourthly (stay with me, there are only three more after this one), a massive, heartfelt thank you to the handful of people who read early versions of some of my attempts at writing books (including my BUG series when it wasn't even called BUG) and told me I should go for it. Like RHONA, VAL, CLARE and EVIE. As my number-one cheerleaders, please award yourselves TUNNOCK'S TEACAKES and dash the expense.

Watch out — it gets a bit soppy now . . .

Fifthly, to my first family.

a. Sadly, my MUM died before my wild and wonderful writing career took off, but I want the world to know that she still inspires me — especially when I need to dream up silly stuff. My beautiful mum was proud of me and everything I did, so I know she'd have been giddy about all this.

b. DAD — the comic who never stops joking despite life's ups and downs. I couldn't love you more. Thank you for everything.

c. My THREE BIG SISTERS, C, J and L, and my BIG BROTHER, B — I know I didn't choose you, but, if I could have, I 100% would have. Thank you for your encouragement. You all inspire me, and I consider myself to be insanely lucky to have grown up in all your shadows. PS I call shotgun (forever).

In the spirit of our upbringing, you are all hereby awarded RICH TEAS and FIG ROLLS (eat up and no complaining).

♥ Love You ♥

Sixthly, thank you infinity (+1) to my massively supportive and encouraging WIFE who has read everything I've ever written, always been honest, and never complained when I've woken her up in the middle of the night to make notes, and my THREE INSPIRATIONAL CHILDREN who have, in their own unique ways, kept my stories full of fun and made my journey to published authorhoodship (not a word) less daunting. I couldn't be prouder of you all nor luckier to be able to call you my family.

Your award is ANY BISCUIT OF YOUR CHOICE WHEN YOU READ THIS (and I won't even make you eat an apple first). (This is in no way a test to see which of you reads the acknowledgements . . . !)

ANY BISCUIT Award

Almost done . . .

Lastly, thank you to YOU (yes, YOU — come on, wake up!) for reading my book. I mean, without

people like you, what would be the actual point
TBH. Your award: CUSTARD
CREAMS for breakfast tomorrow.

Jen X

PS Also, thank you to every single person who's
now thinking, 'Err . . . what about me?' Blame
someone in thank you number 2. They refused to
let me have more than 920 words
for this bit. (Have a biscuit anyway,
though.)

PPS You can clap now.

A CHALLENGE FROM TOBLA

Although Billie, Dale and Layla now obey ELEVEN Biscuit Laws, there's definitely scope for one more . . .

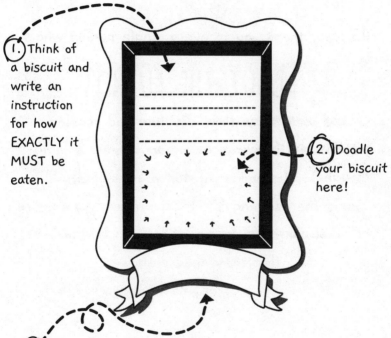

1. Think of a biscuit and write an instruction for how EXACTLY it MUST be eaten.

2. Doodle your biscuit here!

3. Give your rule a serious-sounding name, ending with an official word like COMMANDMENT, DEMAND, CHARTER or LAW.

NOW GO AND TRY IT OUT!

ABOUT THE AUTHOR

As well as writing, doodling and reading,
JEN CARNEY enjoys inventing games, singing*
and standing up for equal rights.
She's the reigning SNIFF champion of Lancashire
and can often be heard telling children**
that they need a shower.
Visit www.jen-carney.com for more details.

*often the wrong lyrics

**usually her own